THRONE OF FEATHERS

KINGDOM OF FAIRYTALES: PETER PAN BOOK 3

ANNE STRYKER
J A ARMITAGE

Edited By Rose Lipscomb

Cover by Enchanted Quill Press

Proof Reader: Tina Merritt

❀ Created with Vellum

KINGDOM OF FAIRYTALES

You all know the fairytales, the stories that always have the happy ending. But what happens after all those storybook characters get what they wanted? Is it really a happily ever after?

In this prequel, you will find out what happens next, be transported back to those lands you fell in love with and be prepared to meet some new characters along the way.

Kingdom of Fairytales is a new way of reading with one chapter a day and one book a week throughout the year beginning January 1st

Lighting-fast reads you won't be able to put down

Read in real time as each chapter follows a day in the life of a character throughout the entire year, with each bite-sized episode representing a week in the life of our hero.

Each character's story wrapped up at the end of every season with a brand new character and story featured in each season.

Fantasy has never been so epic!

READING ORDER

Kingdom of Fairytales is a 52 book series split into thirteen seasons. Each season has a four book story arc of a fairytale character with the last season seeing them all coming together. You can read any series first with the exception of thirteen, however it is recommended that you read in the order below...

PREQUEL

SLEEPING BEAUTY

1. Queen of Dragons
2. Heiress of Embers
3. Throne of Fury
4. Goddess of Flames

LITTLE MERMAID

5. Queen of Mermaids
6. Heiress of the Sea

7. Throne of Change
8. Goddess of Water

RED RIDING HOOD
9. King of Wolves
10. Heir of the Curse
11. Throne of Night
12. God of Shifters

RAPUNZEL
13. King of Devotion
14. Heir of Thorns
15. Throne of Enchantment
16. God of Loyalty

RUMPELSTILTSKIN
17. Queen of Unicorns
18. Heiress of Gold
19. Throne of Sacrifice
20. Goddess of Loss

BEAUTY AND THE BEAST
21. King of Beasts
22. Heir of Beauty
23. Throne of Betrayal
24. God of Illusion

ALADDIN
25. Queen of the Sun
26. Heiress of Shadows
27. Throne of the Phoenix

28. Goddess of Fire

CINDERELLA

29. Queen of Song
30. Heiress of Melody
31. Throne of Symphony
32. Goddess of Harmony

ALICE IN WONDERLAND

33. Queen of Clockwork
34. Heiress of Delusion
35. Throne of Cards
36. Goddess of Hearts

WIZARD OF OZ

37. King of Traitors
38. Heir of Fugitives
39. Throne of Emeralds
40. God of Storms

SNOW WHITE

41. Queen of Reflections
42. Heiress of Mirrors
43. Throne of Wands
44. Goddess of Magic

PETER PAN

45. Queen of Skies
46. Heiress of Stars
47. Throne of Feathers
48. Goddess of Air

URBIS PRISON
BADALAH
DESERT
DRACONIS
ZHORE
SHIPLEY
THE VALE
AZREN
KISBU
MOSA
ABORIA
ELDER
URBIS
AZURE
ENCHANTIA
AIRE
SKYLA
EMERALD CITY
OZ
FLORIS
TULIS
THE FORGE
ARCADIA
RENAIS
W
E
S
MELFALL
ATLANTICE
ANTLA
KINGDOM
OF
FAIRYTALES

18TH NOVEMBER

"The Fountain of Youth?" I stared at Whisper, my brows drawn. The stillness in the air was something physical, and breaking it didn't ease the tension packed within the cramped space.

"Apparently, it's a spring of ancient magical water that gives eternal life to anyone who finds and drinks from it." Her lips curved. "I think we both know a certain forever-twelve-year-old who more-likely-than-not stumbled upon it a long, long time ago. My goodness, it's like this place fills in every gap and question I've ever had."

The way her smile lit her eyes when she called Peter a "forever-twelve-year-old" made my heart so happy I thought I was going to start crying again. We'd only just pried ourselves away from one another's arms, but I swore to myself in that moment I wouldn't let my best friend slip through my fingers ever again. We'd figure this out, then we'd find our way home.

"He shouldn't know it exists," Bay snapped, yanking

my attention from Whisper. Anger ignited in his blazing eyes. "Hook shouldn't have the faintest clue what he's looking for."

"Well, he does." Whisper twirled an oily curl around her finger, scrunched her nose, and dropped her hand. "Mom and I were unfortunate enough to encounter Hook shortly after coming here. She managed to let me get away…but when he had us both, he monologued for a dreadful amount of time."

Still tied to the pillar, Bay shook his head and growled, "How?"

"Some enchantress or something appeared one day less than a year ago and told him that all hope wasn't lost. He could have everything he wished for if he shared some of it. She set him on the right track, searching for the Fountain, but he's grown frustrated. Now that he has my mom, he's thinking he'll use her to force Peter to tell him where the Fountain is instead of finding the Fountain first and using the magic to get his revenge afterward." Whisper set Bay aside in her thoughts, turning to me again. "Wait a second. You said Peter *forgot* Tiger Lily?" She blinked. "*Wait another second.* How were you talking to that pixie? And how did you get here? I have a hundred questions."

"I have a couple of my own." Frowning, I looked at Bay. "How do you know about this Fountain in the first place?"

Jaw clenched, he stared, and his throat bobbed with a swallow. "Is anyone going to untie me?"

"Maybe, after you answer the question."

His gaze dropped to the dusty ground, his eyes tracing the lines the light from the lantern cast over the dusty floor. "It's what I've been looking for all these years."

I'd already figured that part out. "Why would you want eternal life?"

"I don't." Pain engulfed his expression, but he wiped it away. "Its magic offers more than eternal life, and it's not for me." A shaky breath left his lungs, and he tossed his head back to whip sweaty hair out of his face. "Is this interrogation done now? If Hook really is on his way to Skyla with the intent to force information about the Fountain out of Peter, we need to stop him."

"He's waiting on magical resources so he can reach Skyla. We need to save my mother and find the Fountain before he gets them. If this Fountain has as much power as he seems to think it does, we'll need it." Whisper swiped the cutlass off the ground and sashayed to Bay, slicing his ropes in a single clean motion. She pinned her gaze on me. "Something is very wrong. It's not just in Neverland or Skyla. Mom says the whole world has begun unraveling, and I think it has to do with whatever this enchantress is planning. We have to stop her and Hook wherever we can."

I didn't like the idea of meddling in the affairs of a powerful enchantress, but the facts stood. Tiger Lily needed our help, and Bay, for his own reasons, needed the Fountain of Youth. The cave images from the temple floated to the forefront of my mind. The golden spring. Could it have been a nod to this Fountain? Could there have been a hidden message indicating its location?

"We have a lot to talk about." Bay brushed off his clothes and glared at Skye. "A lot."

"So she understands me. Big deal." Skye settled on

my shoulder, the picture of innocence. Bay only narrowed his eyes.

Taking a step forward, he swayed to the right, and I caught him by the shoulder. He threw a hand to his head. "How much knightworth did you use to knock us out?"

Whisper straightened. "I don't know? Why? Is it…"

"Not deadly, no." He took several deep breaths. "It just clings worse than a hangover."

All things considered, I felt fine. I helped Bay upright, turning my attention toward the trapdoor exit. Laughter bellowed through the cracks, drunken songs lilting in the wind. Where had Whisper brought us? My body went cold, remembering the events just before I'd fallen prey to the knightworth. "Whisper, you have my knife, don't you?"

Shock widened her eyes, and her head shook. "I'm sorry… I don't."

A town crawling with pirates. I knew I had dropped it in that alley, but the chances of it still being there were nill. My fingers absently found their way to the empty sheath on my leg. It was just a knife. Now that Whisper was here, back from the dead, things weren't hopeless anymore. I didn't need to cling to material pieces, even if Peter didn't remember me, and that piece was his. I needed to—

Bay fell over.

I blinked at him, collapsed on the ground, then met Whisper's eyes.

She flushed violently in the dim light, stammering, "I didn't know what I was doing. Mom showed me the knightworth and told me how to use it, but she didn't give many specifics."

"I'm fine," Bay gritted, his arms jutting up like chicken wings as he pushed against the ground.

I crouched beside him. "Do you need some help?"

His fists clenched into the dirt, but he didn't snap at me. Looking away, he nodded. "I'm going to be dead weight like this."

"If we can help you walk, and you can pretend to be drunk, I have a room at one of the taverns. You can rest some more, and I can sleep tonight." Whisper offered Bay the cutlass, and he stared at it dumbly.

"In this state, I would impale myself on that. Hold onto it. If we run into trouble, I've seen you move and have a feeling it'd be of more use in your hands."

She tensed but nodded. "I'll hang onto your dagger belt until you're feeling better too then."

"Okay, where's his mask?" I asked.

"In your bag." Whisper crossed to the pillar I had been tied to, retrieving my bag and the mask. Seeing me preoccupied with Bay, she slung the bag over her shoulder and offered him the mask. "Why do you need this, though?"

"This whole place isn't exactly fond of me."

Whisper chuckled. "More questions in need of answers, but one step at a time, I suppose."

Bay released a deep breath, sending a dark look towards Skye. The little pixie on my shoulder peered at his nails a long moment before "becoming aware" of Bay's glare. "Oh, I'm sorry. Is it back into the coat time for Skye? You could use your words."

"I'm not in the mood for this, you little imp," he

grumbled, and I could tell it was the truth. More of his weight seemed on my body than on his feet. If this was how the oil had affected him, why was I okay?

After Skye zipped into place and we'd turned out the lantern, Whisper guided us up and out into the same alley she had caught us in. I glanced at the dusty ground for my knife, but as suspected, nothing remained. Lifting my head to the dark sky, I focused on the barest sliver of the moon to keep tears from falling, then I set my sights on the matter at hand.

Get to safety. Rescue Tiger Lily. Find the Fountain.

Go home.

"Wow," Whisper breathed beside me in the small bed. Bay had already collapsed in a pile of blankets on the floor of the modest room, but we had been talking for the past hour—about everything. Just a few days apart, yet we had whole books worth of stories to share. "I can't believe this place has been so tied to Skyla from the start."

"Neither can I. Do you think Peter has really forgotten it? All of it?" Noise from the bar downstairs blanketed the pitch-dark room in a murmur, and I wondered if this town ever slept.

"He has. Mom said he hasn't remembered for years, and she stopped visiting her family's graves when Dad left. She hasn't been able to fly since either, and she only knows the magic to take her here, not back." Her voice softened considerably, so much so that I had to strain to hear it above the drone of the tavern background noise. "Why do you think Peter forgets like he does?"

My head shook though I don't think she could see me in the darkness. "He has to. He's lived for so long and done so many things that anything not presently a piece of his life gets shoved out of his head." Bitterly, my mind added *like me*.

"Is that what he's told you?"

"Yeah."

She paused, and I could picture her pinched lips and lowered brows as she murmured, "I wonder if it's true then." Before I could ask what she meant, her hand clasped mine. "I'm still coming to terms with the fact Mom never told me she could do some magic."

A dark splotch on the floor shifted and groaned, settling shortly after. I kept my tone lower than Whisper had when I replied, "How can she anyway? I've only heard of people in Enchantia able to do stuff like that."

"People born here have a chance of coming into it, and she did. Because of everything, she never learned how to use it well, but one of the first things taught is how to get home. When our house began to fall, she grabbed a knife, held me tight, then sliced her arm. We were in the middle of the woods before I knew what was happening."

The blood in her home. That's what it came from.

"Isn't it sad?" Whisper asked while I was still wrapping my mind around what she had said. The only magic I was familiar with was pixie dust, and I never considered that particularly special. It had always been a piece of my life, and my island-locked existence wasn't particularly special. Whisper continued, breaking through my thoughts, "My mom's the last true human native of Neverland. Even my blood is soiled."

Her words weighed against my chest with a suddenness I didn't expect. My free hand clasped my right arm where feathers danced over my skin as a piece of Tiger Lily's history that perhaps one she never learned about or didn't remember. Squeezing Whisper's hand, I picked my words as carefully as I could manage. "Your blood isn't soiled as long as your heart isn't. Neverland is full of people and creatures who call this insane magical place their home, whether they've stopped by or lived here for centuries. A piece of the past might be gone now, but that same piece has a chance to live on in you, in all of Skyla. It's *Never*land. The most precious things are never forgotten here."

She chuckled, the sound light. "You say that like you've lived here for ages."

"I'm pretty sure Neverland hates me, actually."

"It doesn't." Her head turned, a rustle of hair the only indication. "I know that much. You can speak to the pixies, and Mom says they're the embodiment of Neverland's spirit. Everywhere you go always wraps around you, like the air itself is giving you a hug. Just walking into a room, you change the atmosphere." She sighed, and her breath fanned against my cheek like a cooling balm, emphasizing her words. "You've always wanted to explore the world, Lyly. Now we have a chance to change it. To make sure important things aren't forgotten. To make sure more wrongs aren't repeated. Mom seems to believe in destiny, but I believe in us. Right here. Right now. Us."

When she said it like that, I wanted to believe in us

too. At the least, I knew I believed in her, and one way or another, all of us would get through this. Together.

We passed around what meager food stores we each had in our bags, from over-salted and burnt meat to berries, to the final crusts of bread. It would suffice for breakfast, and since Bay seemed to be hiding quite a bit of gold in his coat, maybe we could manage another stop for actual food.

I could dream, anyway.

"I'm glad you're feeling better. Sorry about the misunderstanding yesterday." Whisper gnawed on a sliver of tough meat and barely met Bay's gaze. I didn't blame her. He hadn't exactly been the cheeriest person. Airwoman, I missed their carefree banter from the moments when they first met.

He blinked out of his thoughts, glanced at her, then at Skye. The pixie sighed and responded to what she'd said. "Don't worry about it. You can't really be too careful here. No lasting damage, and, hey, you're alive, right?" The smile that followed appeared pained more than anything, and I winced.

"O-okay. Well. What's our next step?" I asked. A bird cawed outside the window, and I froze, my eyes widening on the feathered creature before it flapped away. "Right! I forgot to tell you. Sirens are after us, so we have to keep moving. Do you think we've been here too long, or would they not dare to enter the bay?"

"Sirens?" Whisper squeaked. "Why?"

Bay and Skye exchanged a look, then Bay shrugged. "We should be all right. I've never seen them in the bay, at least." He motioned a limp crust at Whisper. "Our first step is finding Tiger Lily. Then I have an idea of where to look next for the Fountain. Sadly, our original plan of blowing Pirate Bay to high heaven is off the table while Tiger Lily is around, and the Fountain takes precedence after we've got her back. My plan is dangerous. More dangerous than anything I could manage alone, but with five of us...we may just be able to manage traveling to the Nixie Cove. It's one place I haven't picked apart for the Fountain, and it's one place that holds innumerable secrets."

"Perfect!" Whisper's eyes flashed with hope and determination. "I don't suppose you'd know where they're keeping my mom? Or if Hook has a new ship? Since we have his old one and all that."

"He doesn't have a new ship." It took just that instant for Bay to simmer back into his own head. Eyes pinned on the floor before us and mouth still moving, he went somewhere else entirely. "He lives further down the beach in no less than a shore-line castle. Every castle has its dungeons. I suppose we'll find her there."

"They wouldn't have hurt her, right?" Whisper's voice cracked, and she ruffled her hair. "Sorry. That's a stupid question. They're pirates. Of course, they've—"

"Probably not."

Whisper's gaze jerked to Bay.

He met her eyes, melancholy in his whole demeanor. "Unless she's fought them. She's no use to them dead or even injured, and she has no information they could want." Bitterness coated each word, each syllable, as something reminiscent of a laugh left his chest. "This isn't her first time meeting Captain James D. Hook. Not her first time being captured by him either. One might say they each have a certain amount of respect for one another by now. The first time he caught her, she was pregnant with you, and one simply does not mess with a pregnant woman. I'm half-certain, she scared his whole crew shitless."

Whisper swallowed. "I'd worry you were just trying to comfort me, but I'm not sure if that's entirely comforting or not."

Bay stood, stretching, and appeared perturbed that his feet remained solid on the floor. "I'm not exactly a comforting person. We should get moving as soon as we can. We woke late, but after last night's noise, I have a feeling the streets are still going to be empty."

"What was with last night?" I asked, rising. "It didn't seem to end. Is that how it is every night?"

"Not since I've been here," Whisper murmured.

Bay looked at both of us, his jaw tight, then turned toward the door, snatching his mask off a table on his way toward it and running his fingers through his loose hair. "It's an anniversary."

"Of what?" Whisper tilted her head, questioning me with a glance to see if I knew.

The sick feeling in my gut had its guesses; Bay confirmed them balefully. "Of the slaughter. The day the pirates took Neverland as their own."

"Oh." Whisper's response was the last said as we left the room and slipped out of the silent tavern. Several people lay collapsed on the streets, their hands still wrapped around half-filled mugs of rum. The liquor's putrid scent mixed with other unsavory hints of sweat, blood, and urine, and my nose scrunched, begging for relief.

Thankfully, fresh wind rushed in from the sky, allowing us some peace. It was short-lived.

Whisper gasped, halting beside Bay while we crept through an alley toward Hook's abode. I looked up, and the wind ceased.

I had never seen Hook before, but I didn't need anyone to tell me who stood in the lane before us beside a squat man with a red cap. Swathed in black leather and boasting a feathered hat was the very pirate whose defeat I'd heard stories of throughout my entire life.

Unfocused hatred boiled in his black gaze, like tar. It clung. It stained. I clenched my fists to avoid trembling. The longer I looked, the more uneasy I felt. My mind swam, wondering if I'd seen his face before, maybe in a picture, a painting, an echo of a thought.

Had I seen him in the temple?

Bay's back stiffened, all movement leaving him until I couldn't even tell he was breathing.

I wasn't completely sure if I was either.

"He's already here, Smee." Hook tightened his metal hand and swept his eyes over the space before him. "He's already come for the princess. I can feel it." He inhaled deeply, his nostrils flaring above his combed mustache. "I can smell it."

"I-I thought it was because last night someone found the knife he stole from you."

My gaze dropped to his waist, and sapphire winked in the sunlight. My knife. His hand curled around the jeweled hilt. "Silence, Smee. He's toying with me. Just like always. This time, though, ah yes, this time we'll be one step ahead. He has three days to reveal what I want, or Tiger Lily dies."

"No!"

My head whipped toward Whisper as she dashed from the alley. Bay's hand lunged forward after her, but he yanked it back before it left the shadows. Suspecting I might bolt to her side, he stepped back and held his arm in front of me. Panic pulsed in his eyes while they rapidly moved over the scene.

"I won't let you kill my mother!" Whisper stood before Hook, shaking with rage more than fear. No weapon in hand, she faced him down. He made no move toward her, but my heart remained lodged in my throat.

His hand left the dagger at his waist. "So," he began, calmer than he had been, "you found your way here."

"Where is she?"

"I'm afraid I can't tell you that." A spark ignited on his face, some foul realization coming to life in his mind. "Actually, this is perfect. You want to save your mother? Deliver a message to Pan and have him finally give me what I want, then I will let her go unharmed. My battle is, and always has been, only with him."

"Liar!" she screamed. "Do you even realize how many others you've carved through to get to him? Do you know how much blood is on your hands? How many lives you've taken, how many you've ruined!"

I pressed against Bay's restraining arm, and he cast me a heated glare, daring me to push past him. It would take very little effort. And for Whisper, I'd do it in a heartbeat.

Hook snarled, "You'd do well to watch your tongue,

girl." His hand inched back toward his knife, my knife, and I shoved through Bay's meager barrier, snatching a dagger from his belt in a single clean motion as I did.

Heart pounding, I caught Hook's blade with Bay's and shoved it off, staggering back from the force.

The man's eyes bulged, fixing on my hair first, then my eyes. "You," he snapped. "*You*!" He twirled my knife, diving for me with it from one side and plunging his hook at me from the other.

My eyes crashed shut, awaiting the cold sting, but metal sang against metal instead of flesh. Then nothing.

Silence. Silence thickened the air until it was hard to breathe. I peeked hesitantly and found myself shadowed by Bay's form. His cutlass had caught both Hook's metal hand and his knife, sliding them together along the blade until they both sat, almost helplessly, at the guard of the handle. Hook stared, his mouth slack. At his side, Smee looked between them and wrung his hands, anxiety building with every moment.

"Bay," Hook began, an awe in his tone I wouldn't have thought possible. There was something deep in his voice, and though his beady eyes still pulsed with hatred, none of it marred Bay's name, if only for that instant. His black gaze found me, and the moment fled. Hook pulled back, rising tall. "Have you taken the ranks of my enemies, boy?"

"Where's the girl's mother, Hook?" The words grated from Bay's lips, but they came with a dark authority.

My head spun, and I jumped when Whisper's hand found my back. I couldn't pry my eyes off the pirate before us, but knowing she was there let me breathe easier. How did Bay and Hook know one another? In all of Peter's stories, Hook was a madman. Upon seeing Peter, he would lung in with little thought. Seeing him in person, I knew that wasn't the case. Thoughts pooled in his mind, grinding away with ease, oiled smoothly with hatred and a passion for vengeance.

"She's safe. If Pan—" Hook started.

"Peter's not here," Bay all but growled. "He hasn't been here for years. He doesn't even know what *here* is anymore. *Let it go.*"

"He's fooled you too!" Hook jabbed his dagger forward, but Bay parried it easily. "Why will nobody listen? That child knows more than he ever lets on. It's how he keeps all his secrets for himself. Of all the selfish, insipid fools!"

Hook feinted with his blade and swiped with his hook. I gasped when the silver caught Bay's face, but all it ripped off was his mask. The black scrap of polished and painted wood skidded across the street, collided with a building, and came to rest. Hook stepped back, his chest heaving. Looking Bay over, he lowered his weapon and sneered.

Bay remained on guard, cutlass raised and ready, but neither male moved for several long moments. I wanted to speak up, ask what was going on, demand answers to the hundreds of questions I had streaming through my mind. But a lump of fear still hadn't dislodged itself from my throat, perhaps because Hook continued to pin me with his rotting glare.

"Have you been well?" Hook asked his tone no less harsh than it had been.

I recoiled, looking between them in shock.

"Just peachy." Bay's knuckles went white around his

weapon. "I'll ask again, where's the girl's mother? You know how important mothers are to children. How losing one can change a person. Do you really want to make this enemy?"

"Do you speak for yourself or the girl?" With Bay's silence, Hook winced. "You've always had her spirit. I suppose it's no surprise you'd use it against me too."

"I'm not in the mood to chat about old times, old man." Bay's back tightened, but I noticed when he faltered, and his voice wavered with suppressed emotion. "The past between us died; let's not forget who killed it."

Hook didn't waste the opportunity. In the sliver of weakness, he lunged. Metal met metal, but Hook pushed past Bay's block this time, diving directly for me. I jerked back, but he caught me around the waist, clamping my arms to my body. A slice of pain delved into my throat, hot blood washing down my neck, and death gleamed icily before my eyes.

"Don't!" Bay dropped his sword, and it clattered against the cobblestone street. His eyes consumed my vision as fear and adrenaline exploded in my head. Whisper screamed, her hands clawing at Hook's arms. He didn't pay her any mind. He focused entirely on Bay.

Ragged breaths sawed through the boy's chest. "If you kill her, I will never forgive you. I will hunt you down every day and every night until your blood waters the same earth as hers. Then, one by one, I'll peck off each of the minions in this kingdom you've created until nothing remains of you. Nothing. Your name will die in this realm, and I will follow you to the next to make certain it's hell." Anger unlike any I'd ever seen before blazed in Bay's light-colored eyes. It boiled, trapping Hook in place.

Smee dragged Whisper's screaming body off his captain, but her cries fizzled into a void. My life rested in the hands of whatever silent battle went on between Bay and Hook. Bay's single cry to stop had worked when I knew without it, death would have been swift, but Hook hadn't yet pulled the knife from my throat. I pressed my body against his chest, yet with every inhale, my flesh skimmed painfully against the razor-sharp blade.

"Let her go," Bay said, his hand extended, ready to catch me and haul me to safety the second I was free.

"You have no idea what she is," Hook breathed, the stench of his breath unbearable, though the least of my worries. "Does she even know what you are, who you are?"

Bay searched Hook's face, then dropped his gaze to me. I felt helpless and knew how I must look. My hands were numb against Hook's unrelenting hold. My face pale. My shirt, red with the blood slipping down my neck. My eyes, pleading, despite Hook being right. I knew very little about the boy who held the last shred of hope I'd make it out of this alive in his hands.

"You don't need them or Tiger Lily. I know what you're looking for, and I know where it is. All this time, I've been the reason you couldn't find it. If you release them unharmed, now, I'll take you to the Fountain."

Hook laughed bitterly. "You expect me to believe you? I can remove this threat now and have everything else without your help."

"You're right."

I froze, my fingertips going cold, but Bay didn't stop there.

"I don't expect you to believe me. You could have everything else without me if your little plan—which has failed before—works. You could, once again, choose to have everything else without me, without us. Or maybe this time, you could have both for the small price of your revenge." Hook's grip tightened, so Bay's fists clenched. "Hell, fine. Just them. Find and kill Peter later. I don't care. But spare them. *Let her go, Father.*" My ears rang with that word, my mouth dropping open. It echoed on repeat, and I strained to hear his final raw whisper, "Please."

The numb space between Bay's plea and Hook's reply rattled with uncertainty. I hadn't seen Hook before; I'd seen Bay. His son. They looked nearly identical. Heat welled in my head, burning, and Bay wouldn't even look at me anymore.

"I have your word?" Hook asked, his hold already loosening. Bay nodded.

The pirate pulled away his blade and shoved me. I tripped straight into Bay's arms, unsure if I wanted to be there or not as they closed around me, and a trembling breath wracked his body. How could he have kept this from me? What had happened? I was Peter's daughter. He was Hook's son.

And yet, when his arms closed around me, pulling me against his shaking chest, the world fell away. I hadn't just stared down death. I wasn't bleeding at my neck. Panic and adrenaline washed through me until tears stung my eyes. I hit him. He didn't let go.

"How could you?" I choked.

He dragged the bandana off my head and kissed my hair, my temple, my cheek.

I forced myself to glance at him, straight into his eyes. His gaze was tortured, apologetic, and scared.

I slung my arms around him the moment I realized what had just happened, what he had done. For me, Whisper, and Tiger Lily to make it out of this alive, safe, he had traded himself with a promise I knew he couldn't keep.

"Her too." Bay shifted in my hold, nodding toward Whisper, who remained limply in Smee's grasp. She looked between us and Hook, likely the same questions running through her head.

"You've always been soft, Bay," Hook murmured, motioning for his man to release my friend. "I worried about you in this world."

Bay's hand outstretched and clasped Whisper's to draw her behind him after she was freed. "Because having people you care about more than yourself is dangerous?"

"Because losing people you care about more than yourself is enough to break your soul."

Bay squeezed me. "Maybe that's a sign of true weakness. And I won't say I'm immune to it."

"Both of you will leave the bay." Hook peered at Whisper and I in turn.

Whisper shook, but she pulled away from Bay and me, standing tall. "What about my mother?"

Hook's gaze narrowed, meeting Bay's; then he grumbled, "I'll send her to where the streams meet the river in the Whispering Meadow."

Whisper paled, and my eyes widened. That field

separating the bay from the rest of Neverland was what Tiger Lily had named her after?

"I'll make sure of it," Bay added, ignoring the shock on our faces. He pressed his lips against my forehead one last time, then released me from his hold. "Goodbye, Wind Song."

Every muscle in my body tensed.

I couldn't let him do this. We'd find another way. We could take Hook down.

Wind picked up in the lane, beating against the houses and dusty streets. It whipped my hair into my eyes and muted Hook's voice beyond the sudden tempest. In the center of the whirlwind, Bay, Whisper, and I stood in the eye of the storm.

I didn't pay the wind any mind as I reached for Bay, but his gaze was locked on the skies, then a bitter smile curled his lips. He looked directly at me, cupped my cheek with his warm hand, then whispered something beneath the rush.

"What?" I snatched his hand, jolting when Whisper screamed. The wind hushed. I turned my head and found claws buried in Whisper's skin, her feet dangling off the ground. Spindly teeth barred toward Hook, a siren hissed over her. Three powerful wing flaps and the creature had Whisper above the rooftops. I pulled away from Bay, my fingers slipping out of his grasp, then pain erupted in my shoulder blades.

Talons, sharp and unrelenting, dug into my flesh. I fought the siren's hold, but the woman only buried her claws deeper. Warm blood gushed down my back. My mouth gaped in a silent plea, but as my vision faded, Bay stood still. As spots clouded over my eyes and pain boiled in my back, Hook stepped behind his son and glared up after us.

Bay's grim smile melted into a darker emotion when Hook set his hand on Bay's shoulder. The instant he broke eye contact, the Pirate Bay vanished from my sight.

19TH NOVEMBER

There was no pain. That's all I initially realized when I opened my eyes and stared at a flowering canopy. My mind wrestled with the idea that every ache and sore and cut no longer made its presence known.

I sat up tentatively, certain I'd fainted because talons had dug into my nerves, but no ghosting sensations touched my muscles. Inhaling, I choked and scrambled off the soft grass. "Whisper?"

A grove sat before me, calm and gentle. Hundreds of trees heavy with blooms created a ceiling of leaves that crystal light poured through, but I couldn't so much as find a crack displaying the sky. The grass was so green—the flowers, so vibrant. Iridescence coated the world in a fraudulent manner that made me shiver.

I was alone in the place.

Was this a dream? Turning my head, I scanned the woven trunks that made up the bars of this cage. Delicate twists bound the silver bark together in an impenetrable wall. Or was this a prison?

Frustration coiled around me. I didn't have time for this. Bay was in trouble, and he had a lot of explaining to do. Why hadn't he told me something so important? Then again, how could he have brought something like that up? Our parents, since before we were born, had been sworn enemies. How did one approach a topic like that?

I clenched my fists, turning my gaze inward. At the center of the grove, flowers spilled off a mound like water. They pooled in an unusual shape, their colors contrasting the persistent jewel-green of the grass. Crystal light winked off something in the center, and I narrowed my eyes.

Out of habit, my hand skimmed down my thigh, but only grazed my sheath. *Hook's knife*. My knife. Neverland; Skyla. Peter; Hook. Bay and I. We were, all of us, bound together by something too thick to break.

And that's why, right now, while we were apart, we both had to be okay.

I stopped on the edge of the pond of flowers, and my breath stilted in my chest. A woman lay before me in a glass coffin, her pale skin and brown hair flawless. Beautiful didn't begin to describe her.

Her chest filled with air that poured from her lips, but she didn't move, and I couldn't tell if she were dead or asleep. I'd heard stories of curses that doomed their bearer to a state of eternal rest, yet no darkness clung to this place.

Could it be possible she was here to prolong her life?

My hand reached for her coffin before I knew what

was happening. My fingers touched the cool glass, and the chill gripped back, holding firm. Skipping a beat, my heart danced in my chest, leaping up in my throat.

The whole of the dream-like world exploded, falling away as though it were rain.

Mouth open in a gasping cry, I dropped out of my skin completely, something else taking my place in my skull. A wraith's icy touch curled fingers around my consciousness, so soft, but I shook wherever I was with fear.

"My name?" the woman asked peace and laughter in her voice. "It's Wendy."

And then I was no longer me. I was someone else, somewhere else. Memories crashed into my mind that didn't belong to me. They belonged to Wendy...

Chaos ruled this world. No matter where I went, it remained familiar. A breath eased out of my lungs as I kicked the sand along The Vale's shores with my bare feet. Twenty-four years of wandering had brought me here.

To the maddest thing I had ever seen, and I had witnessed the Forge at a distance, eyed all the gears whirring despite the empty, cruel head of the Heartless Queen who ruled there. Nothing compared to islands in the sky.

Like ornaments, they were hung on distant clouds, each of many broken pieces adorned with mist. An ocean of air and water separated me from them, but separation had never stopped my searching before.

Just because I had yet to find my family didn't mean I never would. Just because I had yet to reach those islands didn't mean it was impossible. Even in this crazy, cursed world, nothing was impossible unless you started to believe it was.

So I believed in peace amidst chaos. Kindness alongside cruelty. And magic, above all else.

"Hark, lass," a rough voice called me from my reverie, and I turned to find a man with an unkempt red beard striding toward me from farther down the beach.

"Good morn, sir," I offered, seeing his gaze drift toward the islands as well. "Do you know how to reach them?"

He laughed. "You'd not be the first to peer upon those islands and wonder that. Certainly won't be the last either." Scratching his chin, he sighed, a greedy glint in his eye as he looked across the water at the floating lands. "There's a legend 'bout them. People of The Vale claim one day they fell out of the sky. Before any could reach them, they flew. Then I s'pose only the fae, the birds, and the magic dwellers of Enchantia could touch them if they wanted."

I dropped my gaze to the sand. Enchantia had larger problems to deal with right now. Exploration was a dead hobby embarked upon by few in this age. "I'll find a way, somehow."

The man laughed. "Maybe you would have."

My brows crashed together, but I didn't so much as have time to look up before he covered my mouth with a cloth. Some sickly sweet smell clung to the corners of my mind, and I dropped into a dream.

The world beyond my thoughts rocked. Every dancing fawn and spinning bear in my mind tore into pieces. I gasped awake, but everything remained black. My ankles were wet. Shouts blanketed the tumbling expanse.

"Hello?" I called into the darkness, pulling on restraints. Harsh rope bound my hands and feet to an upright log.

My ankles were wet? I curled my toes into water that sloshed up my legs and against my dress, plastering it to my thighs.

"Is Smee in the nest?" a voice boomed.

"He was thrown!"

The same crude voice as before yelled, "Someone get up there! We need a way outta this storm, or it'll swallow us whole!"

A storm. A ship.

My mind worked as water bombarded my calves, rising. First, I was bound and blinded. Second, the crew was muffled. I was below deck, likely beside other goods the pirates wished to trade. Third, the chances were good that I was alone.

Whether the ropes had been tied loosely to start or the rocking dampness had made them so, I was able to lean forward and push my wrists against the beam until I wriggled my hands free. When I had, nothing held me upright, and the ship threw my body down against bags of grain.

I wrenched the scrap of fabric off my eyes and squinted at the dim cargo hold. The cramped space was filled with water that poured down an open trapdoor. That was the only way out, and judging by the sounds above, the deck crawled with pirates.

It would only be a matter of time before they were down here passing buckets, so I only had now. Fighting the ropes binding my ankles, I broke free and threw my arms around the post when the ship nearly tipped sideways before slamming back down. Eyes wide, I blinked.

I had never been on a ship during a storm before—much less a pirate ship.

I knew the seas were lawless on this coast, but I hadn't expected to run into any trouble. How was I supposed to get out of this one? My eyes scanned the hold. Broken bags spilling grain and smashed barrels tumbled about. I was lucky none of the splintered pieces had impaled me while I was unconscious, but with the water ever-rising and those crude pieces dancing in the murky depths, I knew I wouldn't continue to be so lucky. I had to brave the storm and get out of here first. Likely none of the crew would be too focused on me if the situation was as dire as it sounded.

Dragging myself toward the ladder leading out, I pried my soaking body out of the death trap it had found itself in and peered above deck. Dozens of booted feet clomped through half a foot of water, fighting with ropes and sails that whipped like loose sheets on a clothing string.

Lightning gleamed across the sky, an electric blue I'd never seen matched before. The thunder that pounded afterward rumbled the whole of the ship.

"What are you doing here?" a panicked voice addressed me. I looked up at the man I'd seen on the beach. His wild eyes were raw with fear. I'd thought his hair and beard unkempt before, but that was nothing to the way they looked now. Water rained off his face and out of his hair, spilling through the tangles.

I didn't know how to reply or if my voice would carry through the wind and waves. My head jerked toward port, and my stomach flipped.

An electric blue wave slammed into the boat, tipping it on its side. I rolled out of the hold and crashed into the rail. The bearded man soared over the edge, a scream on his lips that I couldn't quite hear.

My eyes pinned themselves on the swirling water beyond the rail. It spun, appearing more like a galaxy of blue and purple and black than an ocean whirlpool. Angry, it seemed determined to eat us all.

Another wave slammed the hull, and a horrid splintering crack filled the air, repeating. Echoing. Yelled commands turned into screams and prayers. Like a child's toy, the massive ship split at the mercy of the water's playing hands.

We went under.

I gasped air whenever it touched my face, but the choking hold of the ocean wouldn't release me or allow me any say in where I went. The whole of my vision spun, yanking me down, down, down. My head submerged. Electricity surrounded me in jolts of blue and green, but I never felt the sting as each shock lit the water.

Water constricted around my lungs, tightening without restraint. Salt burned my eyes, but in the final moments, as darkness crept in, all-consuming, I didn't see death. Not here in this colorful place.

Something brewed here. Something magical. And where magic as bright as this lived, death had no hold.

20TH NOVEMBER

Heat warmed my skin, luring me out of a deep sleep. I coughed gritty powder from my mouth and squinted groggily ahead. Sand. My body lay plastered against sand. Groaning, I took a deep breath of clean air and smiled before closing my eyes again.

I was so tired.

But I was also alive. Where I was didn't matter as much as the fact I simply was. Still. After so many close calls in my adventures, my soul lingered like it had something important to do.

A roaring screech shattered my reverie, igniting a fire in my gut. I rolled onto my back in the same moment a massive tentacle pounded into the sand where I had been. Ten—or even twenty—times my size, a squid loomed over the expanse of ocean stretching endlessly before me. The creature screamed murder, and the apendage rose for another strike.

I covered my face with my arms, peering through the crack between them. Cold terror washed over my skin.

Blinding and dark at once, a man in a whipping black

coat streaked in front of me, raised his sword, and cleaved the squid's arm from its body. It soared, wriggling, to land beside me in a fury, then limped until it no longer moved.

The creature's red eye blazed, and the scream it unleashed rattled every grain of sand beneath my back. The man whirled, tossing his sword into his other hand where it hung, grabbed my arm, and pulled me to my feet. "This is not a particularly favorable place for a nap, miss." He grinned, his debonaire smile not at all bemused by the writhing mass of flesh and anger behind him. He tossed it a smirk, then we ran.

As we ran, I realized that had the man not come along, I wouldn't have been able to push my protesting muscles to run. Dull pain traced my bones, making each step echo jolts up and down my spine. We burst through a treeline into a forest, but the man didn't stop there.

Wood cracked and crumbled behind us, and my stomach clenched. The creature's reach went this far?

When at last we slowed to a stop, a troubled screech sounded beyond the trees, then the silence of the woods encompassed us. My savior released my hand, placed his above his eyes to peer at the sky, then snatched my arm and yanked me several feet to the right.

I stumbled, my body complaining, as a chasm split the land. Water rushed through like ink, and I stared dumbly at it before meeting the man's patient smile. "T-thank you," I stammered. Now that the threat appeared for the most part behind us, a flush coated my cheeks. This man was uniquely beautiful.

Dark hair spilled down to his shoulders, caressing his black cloak. An icy blue warmed the gleam in his eyes. The beginnings of a five o'clock shadow touched his strong, square jaw. His lips quirked with humor, like he knew I was staring a little too deeply and he also knew precisely why.

I flicked my gaze down.

"Not a problem, miss," his laughing voice coaxed. "I can't very well leave a lady in dire straights."

My breath caught, but before I could look back up at him, sunlight caught metal. I thought it was his sword at first, then I realized it was a hook. A metal hook. Fashioned in place of a hand. I blinked at it while it winked in the light. "Your... hand's a hook?"

He looked down, his brows rising as though he'd only just noticed. With skill, however, he manoeuvred his sword off the curved metal and into a sheath at his side. "Imagine that. I've gone this long and hadn't the faintest clue."

My cheeks boiled hotter, the river beside us coursing with a rush that didn't hide my embarrassment or the thumping of my heart. "I didn't mean—"

"I know." He slipped the hook into his pocket and continued smiling. It was so disarming, his smile. I didn't know what to do with myself. "As I have just saved your life, would you honor me with the knowledge of your name?"

"My name?" I absently brushed hair behind my ear and realized I was covered in sand. I had to look atrocious. "It's Wendy."

"Wendy?"

I nodded. "I never knew my family, so just Wendy."

"It's a pleasure, Just Wendy."

Butterflies took turns doing flips in my stomach, and no matter how hard I tried, I couldn't get them to settle.

"Most people call me Captain Hook," he said, and the mentioned hook in his pocket shifted. He glanced away. "My name's James, though."

"James," I repeated, finally gathering myself enough to offer him a smile in return. "I can't imagine why they'd call you 'Hook.'"

He chuckled, his chest rumbling with the sound. "One of Neverland's mysteries."

"Neverland?"

Straightening, he leaned back on the heels of his boots. "I suppose you are new here. Generally, only pirates wash up on these shores, even though you don't look quite like a pirate to me."

"I'm not." My brows furrowed. "Are you one?"

He placed his hand against his chest. "Do I not look the part?"

"Look it?" I traced my gaze up all his dark leather, past his cutlass, to his charming face, and pressed my lips together. "Appearances are hardly a good idea to rely on. No, sir, you do not act the part. Unless you wish something of me now that you've saved me?"

"Your name and your thanks have well covered your tab." He watched me as though I were as unusual as he, and I self-consciously brushed off my damp dress. Sand tumbled from it in torrents.

Trying my best to ignore the state of my clothes and skin, and the discomfort that came with both, I asked, "What's your price for information about where I am?"

His head dropped forward, his relaxed smile glimmering with mischief. "Must everything come with a price?" His eyes glanced deeper into the woods. "Maybe if you walk with me, I'll just tell you everything I know."

Relaying to me unbelievable stories about the world I'd stumbled into, James led me through the forest until we came upon a small group of huts. He ended his last story with a flourish then bid me find shelter in the village without mentioning him, for whether I saw it or not, he was a pirate, and the natives weren't fond of his kind.

I asked if I'd see him again, and he said, "Perhaps," before kissing my hand and leaving me on the doorstep of a new life. His dark coat fluttered through the woods, fading from view, yet his impression held in my mind, tying us together in a way only magic could.

"Please, sir!" I tugged on my arm and frowned at the two men crowding me against a stone wall. "Let go."

"I dunno, Jack. Whaddaya suppose it is? Ain't seen no bird like her before." The man holding me chuckled, licking his lips and displaying rotting teeth.

I gagged, floating off the ground, but his grip only tightened.

Jack guffawed. "I dunno. I dunno. Ain't never seen one either. Sure pretty, though." Snatching my chin, he pressed cold jewels against my flesh. A shock of fear streaked through me.

Chiming burst from my hair, and my heart dropped into my toes. "No! Stay hidden!"

My pixie friend wouldn't hear of it. He shook his fists and screamed at the men, their wide eyes glinting with greed. One's meaty hand lunged for Skye, so I kicked him in the shin. He howled, though I was certain my poor moccasined toes received the brunt of the action.

Jack yanked on my hair, and I winced. Tears clung to the corners of my eyes. Then the pain died.

He fell, crumpled in a heap at my feet. A knife slid before the other's throat, and his face went white.

"You'd do well to release the lady, Barlow. She's already spoken for."

Tentatively, Barlow's fingers unclasped from around my wrist, and he stammered, "Cap'n. I didn't know— This is your woman?"

"I don't particularly care what you know." James smacked the flat edge of his sword against the man's chest. "On your way." He stepped toward me, stopping when he nearly stepped onto Jack. "Oh, and take this mess with you."

Barlow nodded, furiously tugging Jack away. Just the three of us remained in the quiet lane.

"James," I breathed.

"Wendy." He sheathed his sword and shook his head. "Is this how we are always destined to meet? With my blade between you and some ungodly harm?"

I flustered. "Things were going fine. I could have managed."

"Quite right, I'm sure." He glanced at my pixie when the tiny creature settled on my shoulder, did a double-take, then all his charm dropped away. "What in the..."

Triumphant, I smirked. "This is Skye." I only knew so much because he'd spelled his name out for me when we first met, but James needn't know that.

"It's a pixie."

"Yes."

His lips parted. "But...only children can..." His brows furrowed, his gaze falling to my hovering feet. "You can fly too."

"Yes." I lifted higher off the ground, lighter than air.

His eyes snapped closed, and he reached blindly for me.

"Heavens, Wendy. No wonder those men were on you like wild pigs. Get down from there before you make me do something ungentlemanly."

I'd never landed so fast. Red as the underbelly of a meadowlark, I gripped my dress and stared up at James in horror.

He sighed, peeking to make sure it was safe to open his eyes again. "You are, by far, the most unusual woman I have ever had the chance to meet."

"Thank you?"

"Why are you in Pirate Bay?"

I looked down the cobblestone street. "Is that what this place is called? I went toward the ships since you said you were a captain and a pirate."

His eyes widened. "You were looking for me?"

Skye chimed, annoyed, and folded his arms. I glanced at him to find him glaring at James. "Yes?"

"Is everything all right with the midget?"

"I don't think he wanted me to come here, but of course, now I know why." I smiled sheepishly. "I'm sorry, Skye. But see? Everything worked out in the end."

Skye's eyes narrowed, and he mumbled something else, but I set his grumbles aside. Pixies were fairly temperamental. Looking back at James, I stilled.

Sorrow thickened his solemn expression as he peered at Skye. Memories danced beyond where I could see, but they clung like briars in an obvious and painful way. Meeting my gaze, he shook the thorny spikes off. "Well, if you've come all this way, I suppose I'm inclined to show you around, the brighter part of town, at least."

Excitement bubbled in my chest. My toes curled off the ground, and I took his hand. "I'd rather see your ship."

"My ship?" His expression contorted into a bewildered half-smile. "You want to see that dreadful, old, smelly thing?"

"Very much."

Almost begrudgingly, but not quite, he tucked my hand into the crook of his arm, sighed, and said, "Very well. You'll have to pardon the men before I yell at them, though. We are not used to such fair guests."

He spoke of his ship with a level of tenderness I'd never seen professed by a man before. Wholly enchanted, I wiled away the day—and many others that later came. Though Skye never seemed thrilled to accompany me, I couldn't keep away from the bay—or James—for long.

~

Metal clattered over the ocean, halting me in the air above Pirate Bay. My eyes widened when I honed in on where the noise came from.

James's ship.

My heart leaped out of my chest, and I dove, a hundred horrible scenarios bombarding my thoughts at once. He was under attack. Injured. Dying. Dead.

Skye rushed out of my hair and tugged on my dress, but I didn't stop until I was near enough to see James's plumed hat.

Disgust and hatred twisted his face into something horrible, worse than I'd ever seen. My lips parted, everything beneath my skin suddenly cold. His sword moved with calculated exactness. He was the one out for the kill.

I shifted my gaze to his opponent, and I didn't have a single moment to think. "What are you doing!" I launched myself into the fray of blades and shouts, standing before the orange-headed child with my arms spread.

James's blade dove for me, screeching to a stop. "Wendy." His voice was breathless with shock as his blade retreated faster than it had come.

"Hullo?" the boy behind me floated to my side, a brow raised. Sweat coated his forehead, but he was at perfect ease. "I didn't think pirates had any friends worth knowing."

A furious chime broke the fabricated calm. All around us, a dozen boys, children, stood facing pirates, blades in hand and wary expressions on their faces. Flitting out of the flying boy's pocket, a pixie reprimanded him, her hands on her hips.

"No, no, I just meant— Well, if you'd let me get a word in, Tink!" He rolled his eyes. "I just meant she can fly."

The pixie turned toward me, eyeing me up and down before sneering away to rest on the boy's shoulder.

"Wendy, what are you doing here?" An icy edge coated James's words, and I'd never heard him speak in that tone before. Times with him were warm, filled with laughter. Now, I was chilled.

"What do you mean? I've visited you a hundred times now! What are you doing fighting all these children?"

He scoffed. Scoffed! My brows dipped low in a frown, but his attitude didn't improve. "They are hardly children, I assure you. Our battle has proceeded for more years than I can count, yet it remains timeless." He sneered, "And he refuses to tell me how."

"How?" I looked between them, incredulous. "You know how! This is Neverland! You told me the day I got here, I wouldn't age anymore."

"No, Wendy..." He simmered for the first time, some harshness leaving his eyes.

"Seems like a bad time." The boy scratched his head, nodding at his pixie. He floated off the deck while the tiny

creature zipped past each of the other children, allowing them to do the same. "Maybe tomorrow will be better, Hook. C'mon, men!" He lifted high, pinning his arms at his sides, and crowed like a rooster. Every boy joined him, and the sound echoed.

The familiar sound echoed.

I'd heard it many times before, and the natives I lived with had told me stories about the child who fought in their name. They called him Peter, sang of him as if he were an ancient force to be reckoned. That was Peter?

When they said child, I thought at least a teenager. He looked no older than twelve.

"Wendy," James growled, and my heart thumped.

I ripped my gaze from the retreating children and found him frowning. Weariness coated his eyes, and his lips were pinched with distaste, but the annoyance in his tone didn't seem as severe now.

"Why were you fighting Peter?" I asked.

"Uhm, Cap'n..."

James whirled, plunging his sword into its sheathe and snatching my hand. "As you were, Smee. Victory will come another day."

Without explanation, he tugged me along behind him into the streets of Pirate Bay. "James, where are we going?"

He didn't reply.

"James?"

Still nothing.

Ripping my hand out of his, I floated away from him and crossed my arms. "Answer me, Hook. Why were you trying to kill that child?"

His back stiffened. He didn't face me. "I'm a pirate, Wendy. I'm not a good man. I'm the furthest from it."

Without looking, he opened his hand, palm up, for me to take. "But I will give you the full truth if you want it. I've tried to avoid it for too long already."

I stared between his hand and his turned back. Automatically, my fingers longed for the embrace of his, but Skye zipped between us, shaking his head.

I ignored him. Maybe I shouldn't have.

"Once, I was a renowned captain, a leader of a marine fleet off Vale's coast. Perhaps you have known a better time than I, but in my days off Neverland, there was nothing but war. War and pain and suffering. I'd wanted to change that ever since the world stole my parents when I was a child. I became the youngest marine general, led countless battles and won, until a mistake to approach Elder under cover of a storm led me to a whirlpool. You know what happens after that." James's hand squeezed my fingers as we plodded through the forest. My heart pounded, partly worried and partly excited. He'd talked so little of his past. I hadn't even known he'd come from the same world I knew. I wanted to know him. I was desperate to find more answers.

He stopped suddenly, before a veil of green and stared at me. "For what it's worth, I am sorry."

"For what?"

Shaking his head, he nodded at Skye. "Before the sun sets, I will likely have many things to apologize to you for, Wendy. But in this moment, I am talking to him."

Arms folded on my shoulder, Skye only glared James's way and dismissed his words.

His eyes closed, and he curled his hook in the vines. Peeling them away, he displayed a land charred and crum-

bling. Ashes danced in a forlorn wind. Not even bugs chirped here.

"What is—"

His touch left me cold. The world was cold around me. Fire had so clearly destroyed everything, but it was gone now, a horrific memory of another time. "I am not a good man, Wendy. Not even before I became a pirate. I was a tool, a murderer. Hatred has fueled everything in my life. When I first came here, I wanted to go home. Pan," he sneered, "was the only one I had seen come and go as he pleased. I wanted that freedom. But then I noticed he didn't age even when he left. That was a different freedom in itself."

He swiped a hand over his face and couldn't bear to look at me. My nose stung with the phantom residue of burning wood. My eyes stung for other reasons entirely. Before me wasn't the unshakeable man I knew. Torture and regret burdened his eyes.

"The child refused to tell me his secret. I went to him, begging, but he attacked me. He cleaved my hand from my arm, laughed, fed it to a crocodile, and left me to die." He gripped his hook, trembling. Spit flew from his lips. "I had only adapted to the way of a pirate to survive! But he said one as filthy as me didn't deserve freedom from this prison."

"James..." I stepped toward him, but he moved away.

"He's right. I'm a monster. Look around you! I did this! In an effort to smoke out a single child, I set a fire I couldn't control. You've wondered before why your pixie hates me? I murdered his home, probably his family, maybe all his friends." Breath heaved through James as he peered at his hook. A deranged beast glared back in the polished metal. "It's too late for me to stop. I hate Pan, Wendy." His eyes closed, and his arms fell to his sides. "I hate how he laughed. How he

ignored my pleas for help. How he's an enigma I can't crack. I hate how the people who took me in fear him. I hate how he's glorified. I hate him. And I hate what I've become due to that hatred."

I never thought I'd see the day James would cry. I never knew a man who smirked at Krakens could. But he shook, and a tear traced down his beautiful face.

"I just wanted to go home. To be free."

Skye didn't protest when I wrapped my arms around him, felt his shaking chest against mine. The pixie lifted off my shoulder, hovering above chaos. The chaos that surrounded us now. The chaos of broken hearts and shattered dreams.

"I've never had a home," I whispered. "I've wandered the war-streaked lands as long as I could walk. Like you, my family was taken from me, but I was spared having to know them before it happened. I've wondered what's worse." Cupping his cheek, I brushed his tears away. I hadn't expected the words to fall from my lips then, but they did. "I love you, James. And I love Neverland, even as strange and terrifying as it can be. I have been able to live peacefully here. The world you've tried to return to is no doubt still marred with suffering, but here...here we have the same freedoms as Peter. Time doesn't bind us."

He swallowed, and his eyes still didn't open. His arms didn't lift to return my embrace. "You would ask me to give up fighting Pan?"

My breath held. "I've seen too much fighting in my life."

"You don't believe me. You've lived among those who sing his praises. You believe I did wrong to him; I deserved what happened; I'm a monster for continuing this war as I have."

He wrenched himself from my arms, and I slapped him. The anger budding on his face died. My hand burned, and I winced. "A war is not forged by one party alone. I blame both of you, and I believe both of you in the wrong, at one point or another." I closed my hand against my chest, tearing up from the sting and something more. "I am, however, asking you to stop. To run away with me, maybe."

His eyes widened, and he blinked dumbly. "What?"

"Run away with me. Away from the natives who sing of the one you hate. Away from the pirates who torment them."

His gaze took me in from my head to my feet. "You said you've lived in peace here."

"Yes?"

"You'd run away from the only home you've ever really known, to be with me?"

My chin raised.

He looked over my shoulder, no doubt at Skye. Whatever he saw made him shift. All the confidence I'd known him to have appeared to waver for the moment. "I can't just run away with an honorable young woman..."

My heart plummeted like an anchor to my heels, and I almost turned away to hide an onslaught of tears that threatened to break free. So this was what rejection felt like? It clogged in my chest and choked the air from my throat.

He dropped to one knee.

I gaped at him.

He took my hand in both his and his hook, realizing only after the fact he'd touched me with it. As long as I'd known him, he'd kept the crude metal away from me. When he began to draw it back, I held on tight. Tenderness entered his gaze, and he sighed. "Just Wendy, may I give you a last name?"

"So wait. Is this a yes to running away with me?" I asked, breathless.

"Is that a yes to my question?"

Red heated my cheeks. "Depends. Am I going to be Wendy Hook?"

He laughed. Surrounded by decay and disaster, laughter filled the air, setting aside that era, making way for the next one. "That doesn't have the best ring to it." Rising, he tucked a stray lock of hair behind my ear. "I was thinking Wendy Darling."

James D. Hook.

"Is that your real..."

"Now you know why I go by 'Hook' in my crowd." He rose and moved close, his breath touching my skin. "It's a secret. I haven't told anyone here. Not a soul."

"I won't say a word." Flushing, I directed my attention away from him. "Neither will Skye. Right, Skye?"

Skye shrugged, disinterest in the whole matter etched upon his face, besides disgust.

"Are we leaving now?" James asked.

"You don't have..." As I began to ask, sorrow tipped his smile. Of course not. Neither of us had come here with anything. Neither of us had anything to pack. Holding his hand, I nodded. "Yes, we're leaving now. Skye, are you coming?" I didn't know where we were going, but I wasn't going to force him away from his home. Even if I'd never seen him leave my side for more than a few spare minutes ever since we found each other.

Wordlessly, he sat on my shoulder and folded his arms. My stomach swirled, thankful he was going to stay with me as everything in my world uprooted yet again. In a matter of hours, I'd learned the truth about James, the horrible truth. My eyes swept the scene, and my lips pressed together. Yet I loved him.

Stumps crumbled. Sticks turned to black bits.

I loved him.

Remnants of pixie floss hung across the dilapidated remains of houses like spiderweb. Nothing moved. Nothing breathed. But our hearts beat together, and our hands clasped each other.

I loved him.

Tears in my eyes, I faced him, floating to meet his lips with mine. The touch was cold at first, hesitant, but it melted. It melted and was molten. A heat I'd never known bonded us together. I disappeared into it, for in that place so shrouded by mistakes and death, magic lived on.

I didn't know how to tell him. How could I possibly? Resting a hand against my stomach, I stared at the door. Beyond it, the waterfall rushed, sending glittering light over our home. After weeks, perhaps months, maybe years of exploring Neverland and leaving dozens of half-homes all over, we had settled here in a magical grove filled with pixies.

What would James say?

My breath held when the door creaked open. James saw me and frowned. "What is it?"

"What? What do you mean?" My eyes widened.

He quirked a brow at me and pursed his lips. "The last time you stood there waiting for me to get back from hunting, you'd set the kitchen on fire." He strode in with a bundle of fish and glanced at the peaceful kitchen, sniffing for the remains of some misadventure.

I gnawed my lip, swallowed, and shifted.

Skye chimed impatiently, buzzing between us and making full-body gestures at my stomach.

James's eyes dropped to my middle. "You've...gained weight?" He eased completely, smiling as he went to the kitchen and delivered his catch to the washbasin. "Is that what you're worried about? I hadn't really noticed."

"James!" The man didn't so much as look up. "I'm pregnant. It hasn't even been long enough to show. Have I gained weight?"

He froze, every muscle in his body tightening. Shock overtook his face, and he blinked at the wall above the basin. "You're what?"

Nerves knotted in my belly. "I know we haven't really talked about having kids. I still feel like a kid myself but—"

He met me in two strides, looping his arm under my rump and lifting my body against him. "You're having a baby?" He cupped my cheek, his eyes sparkling. "Really? I know you tease me. Your pranks never grow old, but really?"

Tears burst to my eyes, and I nodded.

"I'm going to be a father?"

"And I, a mother."

For the second time in my life, I saw James Darling cry. The moment of joy lost itself shortly after. His brows crashed low, and he looked at my stomach, tension filtering into the small spaces between us. "You can't give birth here."

I looked around. Though modest, we had created a comfortable home, but he had a point. I knew very little about delivering a baby, and I supposed he knew about the same. "I left the natives so suddenly, but I could return to them, explain, and they could help."

James shook his head. "If you have our child here, Neverland's time will move for them like it does for the natives. We would outlive our baby." Memories darkened his face. "I've seen it happen before, and I'll be damned if it happens to us."

My heart twisted, my hand closing around my dress. "What do we do?"

"You can still fly." His gaze flicked to Skye, and hatred I hadn't seen in so long curled his lip. "Find Pan. Follow him out of this cursed place."

Night cooled the air as I watched Peter's silhouette cross the silver moon. My heart pounded; it had been so long since I'd seen the other world. Hundreds of horrible memories twisted in my skull.

What if I made it, but no one in the war-strewn land would help me? What if I made it, but I couldn't get back to James? What if I didn't make it at all?

Skye murmured softly by my ear, yanking my attention from Peter. His deep blue eyes delved into me, as though he could hear my every thought. So much calm existed in his stern expression.

"You're right," I whispered. "I trust you, and I trust myself."

Together, we followed Peter straight into the sky. My head lightened when I felt as though I was about to touch the stars. Closing my eyes, I shook the sensation off, then squinted ahead again. The floating isles I had seen from the beach so long ago lay before me as they always had .

Hung above the ocean, basking in the moonlight, spattered with stars and speckled with magic, the untouchable land bustled with a quiet nightlife I hadn't expected to see.

"People live here?" I asked the air.

"Sure." Peter's voice made me leap in the sky and spin around. He leaned against the wind, his arms folded. "When the filthy pirates burned down so much of the pixie forest, Neverland wept, crying parts of itself away as a haven apart from itself. Loads of pixies came first, shortly after I'd found Tink. Then I helped the native children who could fly reach its safety. We didn't know how far the pirates would go, and everyone wanted to make sure their families, the future, would be safe."

Though I hadn't seen Peter since that day on the pirate ship when everything changed, he didn't look a second changed. Though, now, his eyes were solemn.

"They were all young. None of them remember Neverland, their parents, any of it. My stories are fairytales to them, and perhaps that's for the best. They've lived in peace off Neverland and away from the rest of this world." He shifted his attention off the islands and smiled at me. "Nice to meet you. I'm Peter." Extending a hand, he sniffed. "Awfully strange to see an adult up here. Why were you following me?"

"I..." Blinking at his hand, I tried to gather my thoughts. What he'd said had been so...sad, yet it was over now, like he'd torn out the page carrying such heavy thoughts and tossed it into the sea. "You don't remember me?"

Skye chimed, and Peter's lips pursed. He pulled his hand back, lifted his green hat off his head, and ruffled his bright hair in the moments his pixie rushed out from underneath his cap. "You don't say?"

Skye chimed some more, glancing at Peter's pixie. She tilted her head, an eyebrow quirked, then fixed her gaze on me, and tinkled.

"I'm sorry, I don't understand pixie," I stammered.

"She says you look like you're about to pop." Peter's brows

lowered with an odd mixture of suspicion and concern. "Did you eat a watermelon?"

I didn't need to understand pixie to pick up the dryness in Skye's tone as he seemingly relayed the reason behind my ample middle. It had been several months since I'd found out before we'd caught sight of Peter. A couple weeks since he'd decided to leave Neverland after visiting. I didn't know quite how long I had left before I would pop, but surely any day now. The only time I felt some semblance of comfort was when I was in flight.Otherwise, I was quite the beached whale.

"We need to get you to Skyla." Peter took my hand, and I jerked at his touch. He blinked at me, nothing but innocent confusion in his eyes.

Skye landed on my wrist, speaking in chiming reprimands.

"He's right. I'm only trying to help."

"And if I were a pirate?" I blurted, unsure where the words had come from, why I would give him a reason to leave me and my child when I desperately needed his help. I couldn't risk losing it. But I couldn't stop my question. "If I were a pirate, would you still help me?"

Laughing, he snatched my hand again and pulled me toward Skyla. "Nonsense. Pirates can't fly."

"If you go back to Neverland, you'll be stuck with a month-old baby forever." Peter stopped me before my feet left the ground. Hugging my little boy against my chest, I turned to face him. He leaned against the tree he and his Lost Boys had built into a house for me. "Some of us can hear his sleepless

night in Aire. I'm not sure why you'd want to prolong this time."

Silent, I stared at him. He had been nothing but a considerate, if prideful, child during my time here. Never once did he forget to check on me. He spared nothing to make me comfortable. So why had he turned James away in his time of need? "I'll be back. It's just that..."

"His father hasn't met him yet." Peter stiffened, age showing only through the tension suddenly in the air. "Tink told me you fell in love with the captain who burned her forest."

A shiver ran over my skin, but I raised my head. "How does she know?"

The boy's brown eyes landed on Skye, who hadn't left my baby's side for even a second. The pixie glanced up, but paid my shocked expression little mind. "Word travels fast between pixies," Peter said.

"He's different." I bit my tongue. That wasn't true. It just seemed the right thing to say. The truth was he hadn't changed. He was still the same man who cared for his home and would do anything for it; he was still the same man Peter had refused to help when he was desperate to return home. I clung to my boy, my sweet boy with James's face and my eyes, and unleashed the question that had been plaguing me since I left Neverland. "Why didn't you help James? Why did you cut off his hand?"

"James?"

"Hook. Captain James D. Hook." I forced my breath calm. "Why didn't you help my husband when all he wanted was to go home?"

"I'm sorry." He didn't meet my eyes, but his brow furrowed like he was searching for something, anything, a

foothold or a scrap of sense. "I don't remember. I do know that the pirates have tortured so much that I care about. When I close my eyes some nights, I see blood. When there's a breath of silence, I hear screams. So when the silence passes and I open my eyes again, I forget. I forget, so I can remember what's important." He nodded at the bundle pressed close to my heart. "Be careful with him. I may not remember, but I know I can fly."

"What does that matter?" I asked, breathless. My heart ached with cold from his words, and I didn't know what to think. I had gotten nowhere closer to learning the reason.

"You can only fly with a very special kind of belief. The kind children naturally have before they're too tall. And you can't trust a pirate."

I let my feet leave the ground. "I believe in love."

His lips curved in a smile, but it didn't reach his eyes. His eyes, in that moment, were chillingly ancient. "If you never forget that, Wendy, you'll always be able to fly. But it would do people like us good to remember that love is a powerful weapon, and it doesn't discriminate whose hands it falls into."

He left me with those words and the horrible sensation there was nothing I could do to stop such a weapon if it were wielded in the name of evil.

21ST NOVEMBER

"Bay!" I sighed, swiping hair out of my face. Neverland wasn't a safe place to wander around, especially as a child. The ground groaned, and I sidestepped a chasm when it split open across the land. Black water churned through the valley, and I shook my head. Skye was with him, I knew that much—the pixie had never left his side since the second he was born—and I'd never met a more responsible pixie, but still.

"He has an adventurer's heart." James's fingers skimmed my hand. "There's nothing wrong with that."

"He's only seven." My lips pursed, but I caved at the mischief lighting James's eyes. They whispered of the little terror he had been when he was Bay's age. Slipping into his arms, I closed my eyes, content.

His thumb pressed against my cheek. "You look older, Wendy," he murmured, his finger running over the lines near my eyes.

"Older by about seven years, I'd say." Cupping his hand, I met his gaze, but it brewed with something dark, and a shiver

cut down my spine. I knew every time I came home from Skyla, I had aged some, but it was only until Bay could make the trip himself and decide whether or not he wanted to. James knew that. I tugged on his beard and smirked. "Besides, you look older too, what with this forest on your face."

His brows lowered, and he sniffed. "It makes me look fatherly."

"It makes you look like a sailor. A fisherman, maybe."

His lips parted to say something more, but Bay's head dropped in between us. Since he had been born, his eyes had lightened into something hazel, wide, bright. Those beautiful little eyes stared at us both now, his hair hanging free as he spun upside down in the air.

"Skye said I shouldn't interrupt." His young voice held no hint of his true age, but his eyes always spoke the truth. "I didn't listen."

"Why you little rascal." James caught him, spun him, and tickled him into submission, all to the tune of the rushing river fault. Laughter filled the woods, even Skye chiming along with us.

~

"I don't like it," James said from the couch.

I looked at him from in the kitchen and found his arms firmly folded against his chest. We had discussed this. "It's good for him to play with other children and have friends while he's in Neverland. I let you bring him to visit your old crewmates. The natives were very welcoming, and they don't know the truth. Even if they did, Bay's a child."

"He's named after the Pirate Bay itself, Wendy!" Standing, he strode toward me.

I continued chopping wild onions. "He's a child. They aren't going to hurt an eleven-year-old boy even if his father was a pirate."

"Is. I can't be forgiven for what I did." Torment tightened the muscles in his face, and his mustache twitched. He clutched his hook. "It will mark me for all eternity. He made sure of that."

I set my knife down. "James..."

"And you!" He threw his hand up in my direction. "Isn't eleven old enough to make the trip alone? Time keeps slipping away from us. I—" Nostrils flaring, he turned away.

I had made friends in Skyla. Initially, I planned to make the trip with Bay until he was thirteen, but then my life changed; I had two: one in Neverland and one in Skyla. Pressing my lips together, I set a hand on his back. "Actually, I was thinking...maybe we could find a way to make the trip together, the three of us? Pixie dust works on pixie wood. If we could—"

He spun, a wild craze coating his face. Between his mustache and his beard, his lips curled.

The door slammed open, jerking us both out of the conversation. Bay stood there, smirking. Held proudly in both hands was a sheet of leather all tattooed with the visage of a ship. Finding us both in the kitchen, he floated over, presenting what he had made. "They're teaching me how to tattoo, so I can be good enough to do Tiger Lily's mark when she grows up." Gloating darkened his hazel eyes. "I made the Jolly Roger, Dad. And look, there's you and Uncle Smee on the deck."

"Well, isn't that just wonderful," James spat. "I'm sure they adored seeing that."

"James Darling," I warned.

He shook his head, ruffled Bay's hair, and sighed. "Sorry. It's well-done."

"Not really. All the pressures are different, so it isn't very smooth. If this had been a person—" He laughed. "—ouch."

James was already heading for our bedroom before our son had finished speaking, and my heart sank.

"Is everything okay?" Bay's eyes peered between his retreating father and me, concern muddling his expression. Just a moment ago, he had been a true, proud eleven-year-old, but now, my baby was once again bearing the mark of his unusual upbringing. A young man hovered before me, already over twenty.

"Some days are brighter than others," I said. "We sometimes have to wait out the darkness."

Skye mumbled something on Bay's shoulder, glancing at me, then back down at the floor.

Bay's feet touched the hardwood. "He says I'm old enough to know the truth."

Bitterness stung my throat when I swallowed, but I pushed the taste aside and shook my head, holding my hand out for Skye. He jumped onto my fingers, and I lifted him close. "That isn't for any of us to decide," I told him sternly. "Please. You know that."

A child may have complained when Skye nodded, agreeing, but Bay didn't.

~

Fire scorched the night, gleaming in erratic wisps. My heart pounded the second I opened my eyes on the scene. Neverland burned. Bay's hand left mine before I had time to register what had happened.

"Bay! No!"

He and Skye zipped through the sky, toward the still-lit embers dancing in the wind. I followed.

"Tiger Lily?" he shouted when he landed on black earth. Wind whistled and howled around us. "Chief!"

My nose caught the scent before my eyes noticed the remains, blood and bone, charred flesh and muscle. I threw myself before Bay's face, but he had already gone unnaturally still. "We have to leave this place, now," I said, rushed, holding his body near.

The flight home, I was numb.

"You shaved?" I blinked through my starting tears. I had wanted nothing more than to rush into James's arms and cry about the horror I had witnessed, but something was wrong. I felt it the second I stepped into our home.

James had shaved his beard, leaving only his mustache behind. With the change, he wore leather, leather I hadn't seen since we'd left the burnt pixie forest and started a new life. Anger marred his beautiful face. But it wasn't beautiful anymore, I realized.

It was cruel.

"It's all gone," he hissed, stepping toward Bay and me. "Everything."

Choked, I whispered, "I saw."

He cupped my cheek, but the motion wasn't gentle. A tear traced down my face, but he didn't wipe it away. He had honed in on the corners of my eyes, where thin wrinkles spiderwebbed my skin. "Peter is gone. There's no hope for us now."

"Wh-at?" My arms hung limp at my sides; my body tremored.

"Out of all of them, he got away." James sneered, his fingers tightening around my cheek until I could feel bruising against my bones. "He refused me again. He left me no choice. All I wanted was his secret. Why could he travel back and forth without aging? Why did you have to? You were slipping away from me; what choice did I have!"

Insanity sparked in him, and my breath grew short. "James," I croaked, "please. Tell me you didn't. You didn't do that. You didn't make that horror."

Jaw tight, he harshly stroked my cheek, hissing, "What choice did I have? Time was taking you away from me."

I stepped back, bumping into Bay, and looked down at him. His wide eyes stared at his father, unblinking, but thin streams trailed down his round cheeks.

"Bay." Hook reached for him, but he lifted off the ground, floating back. Panic erupted in Hook's black eyes, looking at me. "Wendy."

Bay took my hand, squeezing and pulling me back.

"I did this for us, Wendy! So that we could have hope!"

I couldn't move. Only Bay's hand and Skye's dust pulled me back. "We had hope." My throat was raw. I had believed in him so completely. I had ignored all the signs. "Now, it's gone."

Years in Skyla passed in a blur. My health declined.

. . .

"She can barely stand, Father!" Bay, nearly eighteen, yelled. The pirates laughed. I leaned against a house, feeling Neverland against my skin. It eased some of the pain, but nothing could reach into my heart and cool the torture of seeing Hook with his laughing crew that mocked my son's desperation.

My James was gone entirely. I ached, everywhere.

"Please!" Bay's fists closed, shaking. "There has to be a cure! Surely here. Help me find it!"

Somewhere deep within me, I still hoped. I hoped as the man I still loved refused to meet my eye and refused to help me. I hoped as Bay helped me hobble out of the town, north of the Whispering Meadow, and out of the empire Hook had made in my absence. I hoped until my eyes closed, and everything went black.

22ND NOVEMBER

A scream caught in my throat. *My* throat. Lyric. Lyric. I was Lyric. My vision blurred on the scene around me, and I scrambled away from the woman in the glass coffin surrounded by flowers. Gasping pants filled my lungs while images still charged through my head.

I couldn't breathe. I could, but I couldn't. With every inhale, magic rushed through my lungs, with every exhale, it freed me some. A cool wind slapped my cheeks, and I shook. Where was I again? How long had I been inside the woman's head?

No. Not *the woman*. I knew her name now. Wendy. Bay's mother. Hook's wife.

I scooted farther away from her glass coffin, flashes of the burnt natives prickling behind my eyes. Black flesh bubbling like charred meat. Gaping faces and melted skin. Bones stacked high before they had been pecked clean. The scent of it all scathed my nose, and I screamed, curling tight into a ball I swore I would never leave.

Claws dug into my shoulders, swiftly eliminating that plan. I threw myself out of their hold and lay sprawled upon the grass, eyes wide, burning with tears. Darkness coiled around me, around the area. It was night. *When had it become night?*

"Easy, child," the siren before me murmured, her sisters stepping out from behind her wings on either side.

"What have you done to me?" *Not me.* I shook my head to clear it of the fog. "Wendy. What have you done to Wendy?"

The youngest siren folded her clawed fingers before her. "We have spared her. Our Bay brought her to us many years ago, and we stopped her time completely to remove her pain. Only the Fountain of Youth can save her now."

The middle siren spoke, "Only you can save her now."

"What?" My throat hurt, like I had personally gulped the cinders from that night when everything changed in Wendy's world forever. "Why didn't Peter help Hook? Why couldn't Peter have just helped him?"

Sorrow laced the women's eyes, and they peered at one another. "My dear, that is in the past. There is nothing that can be done about it now."

"But I can know the truth now. Why didn't my father help Bay's?"

"Peter does nothing without reason. He sees more clearly than anyone we have ever met. He knows the best of people and the worst. Had he been able to help, he would have provided a strong man eternity and power enough to control that eternity. James Hook was raised to be a weapon in a military force."

The youngest's teeth bared. "He lacks discretion and kindness outside of his interests. The lives he sacrificed to meet his end pile high, as you have seen in both past and present now."

"Whether he could have changed in his soul, we do not know and can no longer tell. All we know is that twice he did not, and the Fountain is not a magic that gives more than it takes."

"You said 'had he been able to.' Why wouldn't Peter have been able to?" My fingers felt numb with cold, though the air around me seemed warm enough. I rubbed the stiffness from them and tried to control my swirling thoughts. They remained garbled, lost as Wendy's mind melded with my own.

"You know as well as we how his memory acts. By this point, Neverland has ceased to exist. By that point, he had well forgotten the Fountain."

"We must warn you." The eldest raised her head, her dark curls spilling down her back.

"Any who drink from the Fountain as Peter has will bear both its blessings and its curses. His body and mind continuously restore themselves, leaving only echoes of what he comes to know. He has trained himself to work with the power, forgetting much of his own will, but the echoes…" She closed her eyes, covered her mouth full of fangs.

"The echoes haunt him."

"We sirens are blessed with seeing the future and the past. Our present is a blur and we have no connection to it. Otherwise we would have met you sooner and warned you."

"You see the future?" A chill made gooseflesh rise on my arms. "Couldn't you have found me easily then? Waited for me somewhere?"

"Without a present point to determine an anchor in time, it is very difficult to accomplish such a task and see what has happened versus what will as well as where we stand in it all." Their eyes closed as one, their faces washed in an eerie night glow.

I swallowed, then my heart thudded, Wendy's memories parting long enough for mine to burst through. "Where's Whisper?"

They didn't open their eyes. "We left her with the children when last we saw her."

"She does so love the children." The youngest smiled her horrible smile, and my blood ran cold.

Stumbling to my feet, I swayed. Claws dug into my arm, forcing me to steady.

"Careful, little one. You've been under a spell for days now." The harsh touch turned almost motherly when the woman cupped my cheek. "We don't mean you any harm, and she is safe."

I believed that, but... "I need to see her. I need to save Bay. We need to save Tiger Lily. Wendy. Skyla." My vision blurred, tears stinging my eyes. "Why didn't he tell me the truth? Why didn't Tiger Lily? I've been so in the dark about so many important things. Am I not worth an explanation?" The realization of something hit me, and my mouth went dry. "You said Peter does nothing without reason. Why did he keep me trapped on Skyla when I've always wanted to explore the world?

Is it still at war like in Wendy's memories? Has Peter lied to me my whole life?"

"No, child. Breathe. Doubts can consume you here; do not let them."

Breathing seemed impossible right now.

"The world has been at peace since your birth, but now you are of age, so war is returning." An odd weight settled those words on my chest, making it even harder to breathe.

"Why do you say that like I have anything to do with it?" A cold breeze touched my hair and cheeks.

Her golden eyes softened. "Because, you have everything to do with it. Magic runs through your veins, powerful magic. Magic of the gods. Unwielded, it allowed peace. Now it returns to your hands, so you must use it to wield peace yourself along with your siblings who were given to the other kingdoms. Once this battle with Hook comes to an end, you must seek out your eleven brothers and sisters from the other kingdoms and save the rest of the world alongside them, else you will never have the chance to come to know it." Those chilling eyes gleamed with light. Her sisters laid their hands on her shoulders, and all their eyes took on the same ghastly glow. They looked past me, past the space before them. "We see your mother, a goddess. Ages have gone by. But we see her and you and Peter. The night is young, the victory, too, when she delivered you to him."

"Stop it." I stepped back, but the glass coffin rested behind me, keeping me from wanting to get any closer. "I'm nothing special. Definitely not the child of a goddess. And siblings? I don't have any blood family, surely not eleven brothers and sisters. Who even has that many kids?"

As one, they blinked and returned to the moment. "You have so little belief in yourself, Lyric. Is it so hard to see how you are a part of a much larger story? Does it not bother you that your entire life has been spent looking up to others? Peter, your friend, the pixies."

"What are you talking about? I mean, the pixies are incredible, and Whisper is so strong. And Peter? Peter is Peter. He's defeated monsters, gone everywhere, done everything. He built an entire country then saved it!"

"With your help."

The very idea was ludicrous. "No, I was a baby. I couldn't have done anything."

"We do not mean then."

The wind hushed, sucked from the space in a single breath. *They see the future*. My head shook, unwilling to believe any of it. "Where's Whisper? All I care about is saving my friends and my home."

"And yet you are destined to save the world."

Anger spiked in my chest. "I don't want to hear any more of this! If the world needs saving, Peter and the rest of my so-called family can do it."

The youngest one's lips tipped down. "He is not as infallible as you might think."

My teeth gritted. "Where. Is. Whisper?"

She sighed, extending a long-nailed finger. "Follow the lark. But remember: you are more than you have allowed yourself to believe. You were not unwanted; you were needed elsewhere."

"And we wish you well until we meet again."

Though gently spoken from maws filled with

prickling teeth, the words became more foreboding than anything else. I didn't want to think I would meet these sirens again, even if they weren't monstrous creatures. I wondered briefly if they knew the stories Bay told behind their back using their name. It got very little thought in my scrambled mind. Sitting in the gnarled branches of the surrounding trees, a single brown lark hopped away. My legs wobbled as I crossed to the slim opening. It hardly looked like an opening at all, and I had to squeeze my way out of the copse to reach dark woods. Packed close, trees blanketed everything, and a slice of fear trickled down my back.

Though physically feeling better than I had since I'd stepped foot in this cursed place, mentally, I was drained beyond compare. I trudged after the lark, finding Whisper the only thing I allowed to remain on my mind.

I needed her sense, her upbeat attitude; I needed her to tell me that, whatever happened, we were still in this together. I trusted her with my life, and I knew only she could help pull my pieces back together, return me to 'Lyric.'

At this moment, what I needed more than anything was my friend.

Her laughter met my ears first, and I stiffened, remembering the changelings and the games they played until I caught a glimpse of her. She sat in the center of a minute clearing, her arms stretched like a princess. A hundred or more birds perched around her, chirping merrily.

Moonlight and starlight—or even just her own light

—illuminated the scene, her smile, her peace in the midst of so much wrong.

When I blinked, tears cascaded down my cheeks, and I didn't think twice before shattering the image completely. Barreling toward her, I careened through the birds, sending them screaming to the trees.

Her wide eyes looked up a second before I threw my arms around her and fell to my knees at her side.

"Lyric!" She laughed. "There you are! I was getting worried, but the sirens said what they had to show you was complicated and unavoidable. What's all this?"

"I love you." I gasped lungfuls of air, but it wasn't enough to quell the panic in my mind or the pictures of destruction still running through my skull. Heartbreak lingered, and I didn't know if it was mine or Wendy's.

"I love you too, Lyly." She ran her fingers over my hair. "Are you okay? I know...a lot happened. And the sirens said what they had to show you wouldn't be easy."

It hadn't been. What they had to tell me wasn't either, but I didn't really believe them. How could I? If I were a demigod or had some awesome magical heritage, wouldn't I know? Have an inkling of an idea? Or was I just that oblivious? And if I had blood family, why hadn't they tried to find me?

"Lyly, are you okay?" she asked when I still hadn't replied.

I squeezed her. "I don't know what to do or think."

"What happened?"

What hadn't happened? Piece by piece in the darkness, I relayed every detail I dared. The love. The betrayal. Peter's involvement in Skyla's birth. The unbelievable knowledge about mine. The apparent future I was meant to protect with siblings I didn't know. Overwhelmed and tired, I slipped into the ending, but it felt more like an unwelcome beginning.

"So…" she began, clasping my hand tight. We lay in the clearing, staring through the gaps in the trees. If I imagined hard enough, we were back home on a night like any other when Peter was somewhere else in the world, and I was in her backyard, watching the stars fall from the sky. "You're supposed to save the world from Hook and the enchantress, and let's face it, anyone else that woman has gathered to her side."

"That's what they told me."

"Well, demigod or not, I think you could save the world. You can fly. Hit a target from a mile away. And not to mention, you've been talking with pixies. Hardly anyone can do that."

"You know three people who can do that."

She pouted, crushing my hand for a moment. "Hush. I'm lucky to know incredible people. I'm just saying whether they are telling you the truth or not, you can do it. And if something like that needs to be done, shouldn't you?"

Her point made moral sense, but not logical. If I tried to do something like that, I was going to get more people killed than saved. "I just want to make sure the people I care about are safe. Then I want to go home. Maybe I'm not cut out for the adventures I've always dreamed about. Peter made them sound so simple, but the truth is…they're hard. You lose people. You see things you wish you hadn't. And the valiant battles between good and evil? They're painful. So painful. And hard." My eyes closed, and I rested my arm across my forehead. "So very hard."

Whisper kept silent for several long moments, then she let a rush of breath fan past her lips. "I guess I hoped you wouldn't ever realize that, Lyly."

"I'm scared." I could only imagine what was happening in the rest of the world. I didn't want to imagine what was happening with Bay. I had seen first-hand how his father could take what seemed like a perfect life and destroy it, abandon those he professed to care most about in their time of desperation. I wanted him to be okay. I needed him to be.

"What happens now?" Whisper asked.

I wanted to go to sleep. Take a long nap and wake up in my room, listening to my weird little family debate over what game they would play next. But I couldn't. My weird little family probably didn't even remember me now.

Through the fear and painful memories, resolve flickered. It was weak, but it existed in me. In Peter's stories, when he crafted a scene where all hope was lost, what did I always ask?

"What happened next?"

And what did he always say?

His dramatic expression flipped on its head in my mind, going from wounded to daring. *"What happened next? Well..."* A gleam shot through his eyes, like it always did. *"I held onto the most important thing I had, and I never gave up."*

The most important thing he had. *Faith. Trust. Belief.*

Maybe things weren't as theatrical and wonderful as he'd made them seem in his stories, but those ideals had been my world for over eighteen years now; they had gotten me through everything so far. With that same childish belief that good would triumph, that efforts would be rewarded, that I would win if I never gave up, we had a chance.

"We're going to save Bay and Tiger Lily if Hook didn't actually free her, which I wouldn't hold my breath about. Then we're going to save Skyla and Wendy." It felt like a lot. It was. But I took a deep breath and swallowed my apprehension, holding how Peter would handle this in my mind because I knew I couldn't do it alone. "To save Bay's mother, we need the Fountain. It's a wealth of power, so maybe we can give it to my siblings to help them save the world, assuming I am a useless demigod, and they exist."

"Why are we assuming you're useless?" I could hear the smile in her voice.

"Because I haven't done anything special my entire life."

"Hardly true." That voice wasn't Whisper's.

I jerked upright, my eyes wide and searching.

Barely visible in the darkness, Skye hovered alone a few feet away, his arms folded and his head raised. "You really think freak wind just happens to follow you around for no reason? You made an entire tornado in front of Hook mere days ago." I stared at him. He lifted a brow. "Please tell me you can still understand me. It would make my life much easier."

Bay was alone. My heart dropped into my toes. *Bay was alone.*

"What are you doing here?" I choked on the words.

He frowned. "Hardly a warm welcome."

"Is Bay okay?" Whisper asked, glancing between us. Sticks and leaves stuck in her curly blond hair when she sat up, but she ignored them.

"He's...in a pirate town with his father, the worst pirate Neverland has ever known, and we've had some really bad ones. So 'okay' needs some specification. He's alive, last I saw."

My gut tightened. "What do you mean 'last you saw?'"

"I'm accounting for travel time. You're a ways north of Pirate Bay, and Hook's blade can be swift and unpredictable."

I covered my mouth, my hands going clammy. "Why did you leave him alone?"

"He said you'd need me more than him right now. I was inclined to agree, and after listening to that conversation, I'd say we were right." His face twisted into something nasty—for a pixie—and he sneered. "I don't care how unspecial you think you are, Lyric. You smell like magic, so *wake up*. If we're going to save Bay and everything else on your pretty list, we'll need all hands on deck—including, if not specifically, your magic ones." He huffed. "Am I clear?"

Dumbly, I looked down at my hands. "But I—"

"Am I clear?"

"No." I stood. "Frankly, nothing has been clear for a while now. You said I smell like magic, so you knew. You knew, so Bay more-than-likely also knew. Yet another thing neither of you told me."

"Like you haven't kept secrets from us."

"Is now really the time to fight?" Whisper remained

seated on the ground, watching, but the line between her brows deepened.

"No," Skye sighed, "it's not." Worry tightened his little body when he looked away.

Whisper stood, brushing off her clothes, then she clapped her hands. "Okay. We need to get some sleep. We all seem exhausted, and we won't do much good while exhausted." Her smile didn't quite reach her eyes, and I knew why: neither of us wanted to sleep right now, but we needed to. Everything in Wendy's memories had drained me beyond a point of usefulness. None of us could afford to be sluggish if we had to take on Hook in the morning, or in the next few days, depending on how far away we were from him.

Reluctant as I was to return to the place with Wendy's body, Skye convinced us it was the only safe place in the area, so we slipped back into the cluster of grass and stopped.

The sirens stood in the space as though they hadn't moved since I'd left. Their eyes clung to us when we stepped into the clearing, and eerie smiles curled their lips. "Skye." The youngest's eyes glimmered, and her arms opened.

The pixie zipped to her, hugging her cheek, and she laughed, cupping her hands around him. "I am glad this future is now. I have missed you."

"How is she?" he asked, his voice small and hardly heard at a distance.

"As she has been and will continue to be until the future."

The younger sirens turned with him. He hovered above Wendy's glass coffin, and I remembered in flashes that he had been her friend before Bay's. How desperate would I be if Whisper were in that case, forever frozen? Eyes closed. A tiny, eternal smile pulling her lips into an instant of peace. An instant that didn't end. An instant that was years of torture for me.

It sickened my gut, steeling my resolve to fix it.

"You are welcome to stay here again this night." The eldest siren folded her hands. "We have provided food to last you through the journey ahead." She nodded toward some branches protruding from the wall of trees around us. My bag hung there, innocently, and my hands felt my waist for it. With everything else, I guess I hadn't realized it was missing. "We have a final warning. When you have secured Bay, go directly to Nixie Cove. If you do not, you will not succeed." Her eyes rested on Whisper, unmoving, until she nodded.

Together, they left, and we settled down to what I suspected would be a restless night.

I was right. Staring at the thick branches above, unable to locate even a sliver of sky, I found nothing but convoluted thoughts to consume my mind. Skye had mentioned the tornado of wind back at the bay. That was me?

It couldn't have been.

I'd thought it was the sirens. At the moment, I hadn't paid it much mind at all.

"Lyly." Whisper's voice was soft beneath the chirping sounds of insects. "Are you awake?"

"Yeah."

She turned on her side to face me, curling one arm beneath her head. "Why do you think they said that?"

My brow furrowed. "What?"

"They said when we had Bay, we had to go directly to Nixie Cove. Wouldn't that be our plan anyway?" She swallowed, and even in the dim light, worry pinched her expression. "Do you think…"

I was already shaking my head and gripping the painted feathers on my arm. "No. No. We won't leave anyone behind, especially not Tiger Lily. She's been a mother to us both for too long."

Whisper forced a laugh, but the tension made it come out garbled. "For too long? Try our whole lives."

"Exactly. Way too long." Rolling on my side, I faced her and smiled. Some of the worry marring her face drifted away, and she reached for my hand. Our fingers linked.

"I've always been jealous of you, you know," she murmured.

My brows shot high. "Of me?" She couldn't be talking about my newfound heritage and possible abilities that I could in no way control. What was there to have *always* been jealous about concerning me?

"You can still fly." Her eyes shifted away. "I thought it was unfair; it wasn't just to spare your feelings when I didn't tell you I couldn't anymore. I was ashamed of growing up while you refused to. But you've grown so much since you left Peter and came here. And instead of losing anything, you've gained the ability to talk to pixies. I've wanted that kind of magic ever since I was born." She huffed playfully to lighten the moment, but I knew she had kept this secret so close for a reason. "And now you're a demigod. So that's nice."

I didn't know exactly how to reply. It seemed everyone had kept something important from me. Though maybe this didn't seem as important as being the daughter of a goddess or the son of my father's worst enemy, it was important to her. And I'd never had a clue. "I don't actually know why I can still fly or talk to pixies. I didn't do anything that I can think of."

"Isn't that all the better then? It's annoying when pretty people know it. You're flawlessly brilliant."

Even lying on the grass with twigs sticking out of her hair, she was still the prettiest person I knew. I smirked. "Look at you, a butterfly calling the moth special."

"Do you even *know* how cool moths are compared to mediocre butterflies? You are absolutely a moth in my book." Her hand squeezed mine, and I laughed. A useless fuzzy little moth, that was a good image for me.

"I believe you can learn to fly again." Grinning, I pressed my forehead against hers. "If I'm going to try to learn completely new magic, you can remember what you forgot."

"But that's not how it works. Once you don't believe you can, you're never able to again."

"That's the kind of thinking that will make sure it's impossible," Skye mumbled.

Both our eyes went wide, and Whisper shot up to look at him in his little bed of moss. "How long have you been listening to our very private conversation?"

"Please. Like I'd be able to sleep tonight either."

Whisper looked at me. I scrubbed a hand down my face. "Since the beginning. Without discretion."

"There was discretion. I waited this long to chime in."

Whisper shook her head, smiling. "Well, he says it's impossible, right?"

"Just because it's never happened doesn't mean it's impossible. I'm worried about her mindset, though." Arms linked behind his head, he shot her a glare.

I rolled my eyes. "He says he believes in you, but you have to believe in the pixies."

"Is that all there is to it?" Whisper murmured.

"Oddly,"—Skye peered at me, a brow raised—"yeah. Easier said than done, though."

Whisper flopped back into the grass and pursed her lips. "Okay. If I'm going to try relearning how to fly, you're going to embrace your inner moth. Is that a deal?"

"How does one embrace their 'inner moth' exactly? Should I begin drinking nectar?"

"Please. Most moths don't eat as adults because they don't have mouths." A tiny sigh escaped her lips as her eyes went all dreamy. "Adam taught me that. Goodness, I miss him."

"She's telling me to starve, Skye."

His chiming laughter filled the space, ringing out through the packed treetops. It eased the pain and loss that lingered in the area, and with it and Whisper at my side, I felt as though maybe I could embrace my own magic—if it did really exist. "It's a deal," I said, closing my eyes.

Soon after, we all finally succumbed to sleep.

23RD NOVEMBER

I felt stupid. I didn't look stupid, hopefully, but I felt stupid. We had been following Skye through the woods all day. As we walked, I continued to imagine magic running through my veins, overflowing out my fingers, and entering the world at my whim.

Nothing happened. The breeze surrounding me felt as normal as the mucky bog we trekked through felt gross. I scrunched my nose when an unwelcome scent greeted my senses. How had such a beautiful grove dropped into such thick woods before diving into this disgusting place?

Whisper kept her head high, but her lips stayed pursed as she picked her way through the moist land. Her eyes shifted to every shadow, every vine, as though she were waiting for something to grab her.

I couldn't blame her. I was just as suspicious, and my hand kept checking my empty sheath for a weapon. It dawned on me a little late that we didn't have one.

When she gasped, I whirled, hand on my empty sheath. "What is it?"

"A moth!" Her wide eyes were pinned on a furry green creature resting on the dark brown wood of a tree. Its wings opened and closed, displaying magnificent red eyespots.

My stomach twisted. The thing was the size of my hand.

"Do you know what kind it is?" I asked, hoping too much disgust hadn't made its way into my tone.

"It's a nosferatu. Don't get too close." Skye landed on my shoulder and held onto my hair to stabilize himself.

"Nosferatu? What?" I glanced at him.

"It drinks blood." His face contorted, though he looked less unsettled by that fact than I was.

I didn't hold any disgust back this time. "Hold on, Whisper. Don't get close to that thing. Apparently, it's one that eats people."

Horror transformed her entire face, and she reeled back, mouth agape. "*You're kidding*. Neverland has ruined *moths*?"

"I didn't say it ate people. It's just uncomfortable, and unpleasant," Skye protested.

"Yep. Come on. Let's get out of here." I ignored Skye's waning look. Something about the moth was creeping me out. "How much longer until we can walk without worrying about stepping ankle-deep in a puddle?"

"Depends on how fast you walk," Skye snipped, fluttering off my shoulder.

I watched him until he spun around and shot us both an "are you coming or not" look.

Picking up the pace again, I tiptoed through the myre, Whisper at my side. An ungodly amount of mud clung to my boots, and every step suctioned me to the ground.

"I hate this." Whisper glared at the ground, slopping along. "Remind me not to build a summer house here."

"If you need me to remind you about that, I don't know whose memory I need to worry about more, yours or Peter's." Neither of us smiled. My stomach ached, but the silent consensus was that we weren't going to eat until we could breathe without gagging. Whatever was rotting around here, the air bore the tale of it with a vengeance.

Something cracked behind us, and I twisted to see what sorry animal lived here. My heart stopped when I peered into distant giant eyes. Clinging between two sparse trees a stone's throw away, was a mammoth green moth. Its proboscis lowered into the mud like a giant straw into dung.

"What is it?" Whisper turned, freezing beside me. "Nope. Nope, nope, nope."

"Skye," my voice wavered, but he flitted right to my side.

"Okay, so that could probably eat a person." He twirled, narrowing his eyes. "You're bait, Lyric. Whisper's with me."

"What?" I squeaked.

He drenched my limbs in dust the second the moth twice my size peered up at us. Its proboscis inched out of the mud, curling slowly. "And fly!"

The creature lunged. Whisper shrieked, running

after Skye when he tugged on her shirt. I barely escaped one long, furry leg as I zipped into the air.

"Lyly!" Whisper's voice carried, pitching with terror. "What are you doing?"

"Keep going!" I yelled, my heart thundering and my blood boiling in my ears. "I'll catch up!" No sooner had I said that than one of the moth's legs thrashed into my side, slapping me across the bog and into the mud. Thankfully, the soft ground pillowed my fall, but the grime covering me made my skin crawl.

The moth scuttled through the weeping trees, and I scrambled out of the way, launching myself into the air. The flurry of weightlessness didn't take hold, and I plummeted back into a splatter of mud.

What?

The creature's wings hummed. I dodged behind a tree when it jumped. Furry legs crunched wood, and all I could do now was run. Dodging through the densest parts of the swampland I could find, I managed to stay out of its grasp. Its wings caught on branches, fraying the edges and leaving glimmers of scales in our wake.

What now? What now? What now? echoed in my head to the beat of an erratic drum—possibly my heart. The mud had washed my dust away. I couldn't fly, and every step was like running through sap.

No weapon. No dust.

Every inhale smelled like rotten eggs, and every exhale sawed out of my chest like I'd held it captive for too long. Somehow in all of Whisper's rambles about moths, she had neglected to provide any information about surviving an attack.

My foot caught on a root, and I slammed into

broken branches and twigs. Rocks bit into my skin, drawing blood. The moth crushed its weight over my back. Turning my head, I witnessed the slow descent of its proboscis.

Screams caught in my throat. All air ripped from my lungs when it laid itself over me. Its furry body leeched damp heat through my muddy clothes. It writhed, settling in for its meal.

Two lives flashed before my eyes: Wendy's and my own. Both tragedies if it ended like this. Mud pressed against my mouth as I sank into the wet earth.

Grappling for anything I could use as a weapon, my fingers locked around a stone. Blindly, I smashed the blunt object behind me, gasping when it connected with flesh and some weight lifted. I rolled, coming face to face with the monstrosity.

Pouring every ounce of strength I had left into the action, I slammed the rock against the moth's eye. The membrane burst, and its wings pounded, sending it backward. The creature didn't make a sound past its humming wings as it flailed, and I didn't wait for it to gather itself.

Drawing myself out of the mud, I turned and ran.

The ground beneath my feet hardened until the slapping of boots against mud gradually changed into the thunder of boots against solid ground. I panted, looking over my shoulder through the darkness every few seconds as though the beast would be back, blood oozing from its face, and hungry for revenge. The bright green never appeared in the drab woods.

"Whisper!" I cried. "Skye!" Silence responded. *Was I going the right way?* Before I could decide what to do if I couldn't find them, Skye's form glittered through the trees.

His eyes widened. "What in the name of the airwoman did you do? Have a wrestling match?"

"I won, thank you." I grimaced, wiping my face. Caked mud covered every inch of my skin, and I didn't want to think what the gritty taste in my mouth was.

Whisper broke from the foliage and fell forward, bracing herself against her knees. When she finally caught her breath, she looked up at me, and her mouth gaped. "Oh, Lyric! Are you okay?"

I was itchy, uncomfortable, and the horrid smell encompassed me like a wet rag. Forcing down bile, I nodded. "I lived."

"Did you use your powers?" Skye asked.

"No, as a matter of fact, they didn't even cross my mind." Flicking mud off my bag, I frowned and hoped the worst was on the outside, and our food was unscathed. I stopped, looking at Skye. "Is that why you left me like that? You wanted me to use powers I have no idea how to control?" My voice rose. "I could have died!"

He held up his hands, blue eyes wide. "It was an afterthought, I promise."

Huffing, I glared, then looked away. "Fine. Sorry."

"Did its legs touch you?" Whisper lifted my pinky between two fingers to raise my arm. "Normal moths have hair on their legs that can irritate the skin. I can only imagine what that..." Her lips pursed. "Never mind. I don't have to imagine."

I followed her gaze to my side where my shirt had been shredded straight through my vest. Mud and red coated my skin, and purple darkened whatever I could see. I shivered.

"That needs to be cleaned, and we need to rest if we're going to have any chance of rescuing Bay." Skye winced, staring off in the distance. My thoughts wandered to the same place. We couldn't afford any setbacks. Bay needed us. Skye shook his head, nodding off-course. "There's a native settlement in that direction. It's tiny compared to the others, but it will have a water source and a change of clothes."

The thought of a bath was almost too much, but my head shook. "I'll be fine for a day; we can eat and rest up ahead."

"No, we won't."

"What's he saying?" Whisper folded her arms. "If he thinks that we're going to continue without cleaning that—"

"He's thinking just the opposite. But Bay—"

Whisper set her hands on her hips and stared down her nose at me. "Bay can and will handle himself for the extra hour or so it takes to make sure you aren't going to get an infection or some magical Neverland disease."

Skye nodded, though I could see the reluctance on his face. "Bay told me specifically to make sure you would be okay." When his gaze shifted away, my heart thudded.

"He told you to take us back to Skyla, didn't he?" With all that happened during the encounter with Hook, I hadn't seen it, but thinking back, it was so clear. Bay had said goodbye. "Didn't he?" I repeated, sterner.

"None of us would have been happy with that." The statement held no bitterness, no ire. We both knew it was true. Skye hadn't guided us to this point against our will. I'd mentioned saving Bay before he'd even said a word; it had never been—even for a second—an option to overlook.

"Okay." I hoped to heaven Bay hadn't given up and taunted Hook into doing something irreversible. "Clean up. Get back on track. When will we make it there?" My side stung, but I gritted my teeth against the pain. By now, I was used to Neverland's attacks.

"Tomorrow afternoon. No later, if nothing else goes wrong."

Nodding, I turned to Whisper. "Tomorrow afternoon."

She peered up at the sky and squinted. The cheerful blue mocked what had just happened, the near-death I'd just experienced, and a breath fanned past her lips. "Okay, let's get going."

24TH NOVEMBER

We had planned our rescue mission from outskirts of the woods until sunset had poured over the bay, painting it in shades of blood and orange. Beneath the bandages Whisper had wrapped around my waist, the cuts burned, making me disinclined to move, but on the surface, I appeared ready to fight.

Worn and long-forgotten clothes from one of Hook's other victims caressed my skin, providing me with even more reasons to battle with everything I had. His reign had tormented too many for too long, and it was time to end it.

"The whole town will be looking for you two," Skye murmured near my ear. He hadn't left my shoulder since we'd broken from the trees and seen the bay at a distance. "We'll have to keep to the shadows and ease our way to Hook's castle. I really don't know how we're going to pull this off."

I looked at him when he scrubbed a hand down his

face. I'd never known any of the pixies to be quite as expressive as him. Tinkerbell was flighty, vain, and the tiniest bit motherly when she felt like it. The ancient, magical creatures seemed more like glorified children than anything else. No childishness crossed Skye's eyes, only worry, pain, and fear.

"Maybe I can remember how to fly?" Whisper asked, determination lighting a fire in her gaze. "If I can fly, we'll have a better chance."

Skye wordlessly lifted off my shoulder and flew several circles around her head. Dust settled in her hair, glimmering against the blond locks. She took a breath, closed her eyes, and…nothing.

"There's a good chance we'll be able to find a sword along the way." Skye returned to the matter at hand without missing a beat. "Drunk pirates tend to lose those things right before they lose their heads."

Whisper's face fell, and she turned inward. Her small voice stung almost as bad as my cut. "What's he saying?"

"You're relying on the wrong thing." I took her hand, feeling some of Skye's dust had touched my hair and neck. It wasn't much, but it would be just enough for a second. "You can't do it if you just rely on yourself. You have to believe in it, let it carry you." My feet left the ground; hers remained planted firmly in place.

"I hardly know him. How am I supposed to do that?" Her fingers nearly slipped out of mine, so I held tighter. "I've seen you go too high and fall before, Lyly. What if—"

"I may have fallen before, but I've never hit the ground. No matter what, even though they are so *pissed* with me, a pixie always catches me." I shrugged a shoulder. "They're pixies, Whisper. They love children and games and laughing. They don't like to see pain or fear."

"We're darling incarnate." Skye's wry smile caught my eye, and I sighed.

"If you don't believe in him, believe in me."

Her gaze dropped to our hands, then she let out a deep breath. Tension tightened the lines between her brows, and I wanted to tell her she was concentrating too hard. Flight was effortless; it had to be, but she was trying so hard, and I didn't want to interrupt.

Ripping her hand out of mine, she shook her head. "I'm sorry. I can't." She didn't meet my gaze as she turned her back on me. Her shoulders, always pulled back, caved in on herself. "I just can't."

My feet returned to the ground, and I bit my cheek, my heart sinking. "It's okay," I said, but it didn't feel okay. "We'll get through this, and, hey, Bay's been flying a lot longer than I have. Maybe he can help."

Without a word, she nodded, and we turned to face the endless sea.

"Let me go!" I spat, my heart stampeding. We hadn't even made it into the town before pirates surrounded us. Skye hid in my bag, so they hadn't seen him yet, but that didn't change the fact that a tiny pixie could do very little to help us.

The man holding Whisper yelped when her heel swung back into his shin, but the victory ended in her scream as he caught her by the hair and tugged her head down. "Sit still, you little bitch," he hissed.

"Where are you taking us?" She gritted her teeth

against the pain, fury clear on her face even in the darkness. Torches flickering in the lanes did very little to illuminate the roads as they took us through one alley after another.

I could hardly count them. There may have been ten men, twenty? We hadn't stood a chance.

"Cap'n Hook is busy. His order of magic came in, so where should we take 'em until he gets back?"

The man holding me shrugged, his hold never loosening even with the action. "Might as well throw them in with the other brat. I doubt they'll be able to get up to much trouble, all things considered."

The laughter that followed made me pale. *What had they done to Bay?*

Glancing at Whisper's face in the dimness, I saw she had a very different thought. Her wide eyes glassed like tears were about to fall, and her lips parted, mouthing a single word to no one in particular. *Mom.*

I didn't want to know, but I would very soon. My stomach lurched with every step that brought us down winding stairs into the maws of a dungeon. It smelled no better than the bogs we'd only just escaped the night before, but the hints of iron cutting through the musk were what terrified me more than anything else.

The creak of an old metal door broke my thoughts, then pain erupted on my side, splitting my scars anew as a pirate threw me into the cage. Warm blood gushed, and I curled in on myself while Whisper crashed in beside me. She didn't allow pain a second to hold her as she scrambled back to her feet and hissed at the men, teeth bared and feral.

The gate closed, their sneers and laughter drifting

away. Whisper whirled to my side once the noise had faded out of earshot. "Lyly," her hands hovered near me, "can you breathe?"

Every inhale was a shot to the gut. It felt as though my flesh had been ripped open, torn further than before like cloth. Lip quivering against my will, I nodded. She clasped my outstretched hand, squeezing it to help me balance the pain, then her head whipped in all directions, searching for her mom in the shadows. With every second, her expression dropped deeper into hopelessness.

"Skye," I choked, trying to move my body in a way that would allow my bag more mobility. I thanked the airwoman I hadn't landed on it, but surely he'd been jostled inside. Whisper helped me open the flap, and the little pixie zipped out, paying us no mind at all.

"Bay." The soft word made my heart skip a beat. I followed Skye's trail to a crumpled figure in the corner and crushed Whisper's hand. In the bare light from a single torch outside the cell, I could see swollen flesh and battered, purple skin. One eye was swollen shut; the other hadn't opened, despite all the noise the pirates had made when they'd thrown us in here.

For a second, I thought he was dead; we were too late. All the pain in my gut vanished. I pulled myself up, desperate to reach him and discover the truth.

"Lyly!" Whisper tried to stabilize me, but I broke from her hands and made it to Bay's side. Things were so much worse up close. My breath entered and left me in erratic gasps as I scanned his torn skin and clothes. Blood painted his open shirt, and the massacre continued down his chest. Dozens of thin lashes bloomed with beads of red like he'd been whipped just minutes ago.

Tears sprung to my eyes. "Bay…" Shaking, my hand reached for him, but my gaze dropped when his chest stuttered with an inhale.

"Is he…" Whisper didn't finish the question.

"He's alive," I choked on the words, closing my eyes and trapping the tears waiting to fall. "He's alive."

"What have they done to him…" Skye's fists clenched as he landed on Bay's shoulder and examined his swollen eye. One of his lips was split, and a stray hair was caught in the blood. Gently, I pushed it back over his ear and stopped when gold gleamed in the firelight.

An earring, like those so many of the pirates had, protruded from his lobe. The metal was stained with dried blood, rust, and grime. How could they? *How dare they*? Wind rushed down the line of cells, swirling the fire and feeding it into a blaze. My hands shook. My side stung.

Dust fled the wind, the all-consuming air, but rocks fled it too. It only stopped when Whisper squeaked. "Careful!"

The wind died, and I looked at her. She sat curled behind me, covering her face, and a rock skidded to a stop behind her. When she met my gaze, a laugh bubbled out of her.

"I didn't mean to," I stammered, dropping my attention to my hands. "I…"

"You can't control it, but dang if you don't have it, Lyly!" She attempted to tame her hair, but our journey plus the wind just now made such a thing no less than impossible. I didn't even want to know what my hair looked like. "We may just have a chance."

I looked back at Bay. "Not if he doesn't wake up. Not if he can't walk."

"He'll be fine," Skye said, planting himself on Bay's shoulder. "He's come out of worse."

I looked him over, from every cut to every oozing wound, and the thought of that made me sick. The sickness tightened in my stomach, pulling on my own superficial injuries, so I set a hand against them and adjusted myself near his side. As carefully as I could manage, I removed the earring marking him as a pirate and thrust it away.

There was no hope of my falling asleep in this dungeon with the smell of blood so thick in the air. I tried desperately to pull a clean breeze into the room, but no matter how hard I tried, nothing happened. A great help powers were when you had no control over them...

We had decided to wait until Bay woke up, getting some rest ourselves in the meantime before we attempted escape, but only Whisper and Skye seemed to have managed in the "rest" department. I couldn't stop blaming myself. If only he hadn't sacrificed himself for us. If only he hadn't taken me to Pirate Bay at all. If only he'd open his eyes.

I traced his jaw with my fingers, focusing on a dark bruise. What father could do this to their child? What person could do this to anyone? I had seen Hook in love. I had seen him in pain, anguish even. How could he find it in himself, knowing that pain, to bring anything like it upon others? Upon his own flesh and blood?

My soul ached for Wendy.

Bay's face twitched, his brow deepening, and my heart rate picked up. His groan barely made a sound as he shifted his weight. Just as soft, a stream of curses befitting his heritage tumbled past his lips in a fluidly skillful manner that made me blush. Unsure what to do, I waited for him to crack open his good eye. When he did, he saw me. I waited for him to respond, yell, say everything he'd gone through meant nothing now that I was here, but he barely acknowledged my presence, simply mumbling, "Great."

"I'm sorry?" I meant the apology; I hadn't intended for it to come out as a question.

"Still dreaming," he grumbled, "which means this pain is a hell of a lot worse than it already feels."

I wasn't sure how to reply to that. I was flattered he thought I looked like a vision from his dreams—because I knew that a scullery-maid-who-had-been-working-in-a-coal-mine was a more appropriate description.

"Can't you give me a break?" He coughed, and his whole being winced with regret at the action. Despite that, he continued, "I'd expected nightmares, or my mother, to haunt me, but you won't leave me alone." He narrowed his good eye at me in accusation. "Is this how bad it's gonna be missing you, Wind Song?" He lifted his arm, cupping my cheek, and my breath held completely. So completely that the wind in the whole room stilled. Even the fire didn't so much as flicker. "We've only known each other for a few weeks. You'd think I'd be able to let this shit go."

"I know I wouldn't be able to," I whispered.

He smiled, his thumb running over my cheek. "If I had half a mind right now, I'd tell you I loved you, but I can barely feel half my body."

My eyes widened, and my lips parted. No words escaped them. In my chest, my heart erupted, pounding in my ears, and I knew hot red covered my cheeks.

Bay's smirk widened as if he'd noticed. "Maybe I won't wake up from this one. If I can stay here with you, I think I'd like to."

Stay here with me. In pain, in a dingy cell. And yet it was worth it because I was with him? I shook my head. He was delirious, beaten within an inch of his life. And I was tired—clearly. There were a hundred more important things to dwell on right now. "Bay,"—I sterned my voice, hoping I'd tossed away the enchantment he had over me—"this isn't a dream. We have to get out of here. Right now, Hook is gone. We need to leave before he comes back." My eyes dropped to his chest, and I pulled them away before they could linger. "Do you think you can walk?"

He blinked dumbly, his smile fading, and I thought surely now he'd yell if he had the energy to do so. He tapped my cheek twice, dropped his hand, and looked away. "Are you serious?"

"Yes?" I gnawed my cheek.

"So, I lived. That's always a nice surprise." He looked himself over, disgust curling his split lip. "Okay, that's less nice. But living. Love when I live."

"Are you...okay?" I don't know why I asked. Physically, definitely not. Mentally, he'd just said he'd loved me, so also no.

"Just fine. Where's Skye? I can't walk. Might have a broken rib, but I'll be damned if I can't fly. Literally. We're damned if I can't fly." Though said in Bay's usual lighthearted manner, the weight of those words settled in my gut. As if aware, he glanced at me, the brow above his swollen eye jumping. "Don't look so worried, Wind Song. I've never not been able to fly."

There were a million things to worry about right now. Even if he could walk, we were still in a cell. Who knew how many pirates were waiting at the mouth of this dungeon to catch us if we managed to get that far. No sign of Tiger Lily either. Maybe before everything had happened, Hook kept his word and released her?

I could only hope.

Whisper shifted, squinting, then she gasped. "He's awake. Thank the airwoman." Easing into an upright position, she stretched, her back popping audibly. "Ugh. I don't want a summer home here either."

Skye stirred shortly after Whisper, blinking drearily as he floated off the ground. Sleep left him the second he saw Bay, and he darted in to hug his cheek.

Bay hissed as the tiny body collided with his bruises, but he didn't complain. "I thought I said, very clearly, 'make sure they make it back home'?"

"What good does being on Skyla do if the world is ending?" Skye grumbled.

"We weren't going to leave you." I held his gaze. "That would never have been an option." *And,* I wanted to add, *you could have told me the truth. I would have helped you.* But I left those words unsaid.

"So," Whisper broke the moment, "how do we get

out of here? And find my mom? And get to Nixie Cove?"

"One thing at a time," Bay started. His mouth closed halfway through what he was saying, and I raised a brow. His attention fell to the ground, as though he were searching for something, then he looked into the cell next to ours. "Well, one less thing at a time. Your mom is probably searching for you in Neverland by now. We'll have to find her once we get out of here."

Whisper sighed with relief, her eyes sparkling. "Thank you, Bay." She looked him over. "For everything you did to make sure she was freed."

He stiffened. "Don't thank me. I haven't done anything for you. Really."

Most people may have been hurt by such words, but Whisper only smirked, sending me a wink. "Well, then."

"How are we going to get out of here?" I asked, pushing aside my friend's comments. We weren't in any position to be distracted by red faces and pounding hearts.

"Easy. I'll smash the lock with the rock that nearly smashed me, then when we get up the stairs, you can blow everyone out of the way. We'll make a mad dash, get to the cove, save the world, and go home in time for my moth prince and me to have a charming honeymoon."

Bay glanced between us. "I guess you know about your magic stuff now?"

"There is no magic stuff," I frowned. *So he had known. And no one thought to tell me.* "If there is, I can't do anything with it, so there isn't."

"You knew she was a demigod?" Whisper's eyes widened.

Shock twisted Bay's already mangled face. "A demigod? What? No. I figured she had magical heritage, probably a sylph."

"Surprise! It was a goddess." Whisper giggled. "Maybe the airwoman herself. I'm going to start saying, 'Oh, my Lyric' from now on."

"Please don't." I pulled my legs against my chest and held a hand at my wounds. "We need a better plan. We can't rely on me."

Bay stretched his left arm, and I noticed he hadn't moved his right one since he'd woken up. "In that case, we may just have to pull a Peter."

"What's that mean?" I asked.

Silently, Skye pinned his arms at his sides, and twirled into the air, imitating Peter's crow. He smirked at Bay, then all three of us ended up heavily dusted. Bay floated to his feet, not quite landing on them.

"When we get the signal, we have to move. The second we're in the air, they won't be able to get us."

"One problem." Whisper raised one hand and bit her lip.

"Right." Bay pointed at her. "Right. Okay..."

"Could we pull a moth?" Skye grinned at me.

My nose scrunched when Bay quirked a brow in my direction. "A moth?"

"We'd be the diversion, so Whisper can get away under their noses." I rubbed my side and sighed. "It went passably well last time."

"Diversions, we can do, right, Skye?"

"I'll rally the forces. Give me an hour." He fluttered

toward the iron bars, then turned and pointed at me. "Don't lose your dust this time. And, Bay, save yours."

Obediently, Bay settled back against the wall and raised his good hand. "Fine, fine. As for you." His expression darkened. "Don't get caught."

Waiting was torture. Sitting cross-legged, I watched my knee bounce. Bay relaxed against the back wall, his skin shimmering with dust and bruises. How much pain was he in? He seemed so at peace in the face of so much danger. "How often does this happen?" I asked.

"What do you mean?" He didn't open his eyes.

"She means you're sitting there like it's an average day in Neverland." Whisper glanced down the quiet dungeon hall. "Which isn't actually hard to believe."

"I don't feel well enough to panic." His chest moved slowly, each breath a tedious effort.

"What if Hook gets back before Skye can make it?" Whisper turned toward the stairs that led out of this place. "What if Skye didn't make it at all?"

"Then we're doomed." Bay didn't bother with sugar-coating, though he didn't appear ruffled by the notion.

I frowned. "He'll make it. We only have to worry about whether or not we will."

"I'm certain I can break the lock. This place doesn't look like it's been used for years. It's practically falling apart on its own." Her nose wrinkled. "Not that I'm complaining."

She was right. The whole place was old, musty, and vacant. Perhaps the last part was the only real indication it hadn't been used in a while. Old and musty were nearly requirements for a dungeon, but empty was not.

"No Lost Boys and no natives. In a lawless land, who are the only people worth throwing in jail?"

Looking at Bay, I knew the answer. *People you wanted to make pay,* To *torture.*

Bay took a deeper breath, letting it out slowly. "Anyway, they're all gone now."

What would Neverland have looked like now had the pirates not taken over completely? Would the terrain still be as treacherous? Or would the people living here have known how to navigate it in a way that tamed the wonderland to their will?

Shouts sounded above, feet stampeding. Bay smirked, lifting off the ground. His hazel eyes opened, and they sparked with determination. Distantly, crows sounded, overlapping. They repeated, louder.

"At the ready, men," Bay said, not unlike Peter would have. The mix of nostalgia and his infectious spirit made my racing heart believe we had a chance.

I nodded at Whisper, and she lifted the rock. The lock trapping us here came undone with her second hit, and she tossed the screeching door open. Grinning, she dropped the rock, but before it could hit the ground, Bay snatched it with his left hand and tossed it up, gliding through the air on his back. "Waste not, want not."

Adrenaline pounded through my veins as I floated. "What exactly is Skye doing up there?" It sounded like an army had come to our defense.

"He called in a couple favors from a couple friends. We should really get moving." Bay wore his pain well as he slipped out of the cage, but something about the form of his flight wasn't right. Instead of his body moving with the air, he skimmed through it, rigid. To watch it felt wrong.

The sooner this was behind us, the better.

Snatching my own rock off the ground, I nodded at Whisper. "Make sure the way is clear and keep to the shadows."

"If you need help, we have your back," Bay added.

Her gaze clung to our elevated feet for a brief moment, then she smiled; it didn't reach her eyes. "Got it."

We began our ascent. The noises got louder. Yells and chiming laughter mixed with familiar crows as we flew out of the dungeon into a mad fog of pixies and pirates.

"Well," Bay said, diving into the air above the pirates and dropping his rock on one of their heads, "this will do nicely." He plucked a floating sword out of some pixies' hands, examined the blade, then looked at me. "Want one?"

The mindless scramble around me, the endless noise, the pain in my side, and yet I laughed. "A dagger if you can," I replied, slipping to the side when a pirate lunged for me.

"You heard the lady." He motioned extravagantly toward the pixies, several of them giggling and saluting before rushing off. His bruised face didn't look any less handsome from this angle, or maybe it was his spirit I found myself attracted to. Whatever it was, my mind wandered during the fray to his earlier words. *If I had half a mind right now, I'd tell you I loved you.* Only

Whisper had ever told me she loved me before. It was a statement unbefitting of Peter, though I liked to think he showed it sometimes, and Tiger Lily said a good number of things with her eyes instead of her mouth.

I dodged out of the way of someone's blade, glancing behind me to see if Whisper had made it out. She was nowhere to be seen, so I had to hope she was well on her way.

We'd make sure we got the best of these scallywags, then we'd meet up, and the adventure would continue. In the rush, I almost forgot all the bad things. Following Bay's lead, I twirled and dove and danced. The pixies snagged me a dagger, and it joined the ballet of singing metal.

"You appear in your element." Bay sidled up beside me, deflecting a jab.

I glanced at him, and the thrill of everything dimmed. Sweat drenched his brow, and his blood-matted hair stuck to his face. With every attack, vibrations ran through his broken body, accentuating every shred of pain.

"I think it's time for both of us to immerse ourselves in the elements." I motioned with my eyes to the cloudy sky. He caught what I meant and tucked his sword in his belt before snatching my arm and pulling me out of reach. Daggers came flying, but when I saw them and gasped, a strong wind plowed them off track.

When we were high enough that fog consumed us, Bay released me, stuck his fingers in his mouth, and unleashed a shrill whistle. Shortly after, Skye popped into our cloud, arms folded and frowning. "I am not a dog," he stated before providing Bay a fresh coat of dust.

During the battle, the pixies had each taken their turn showering us, so I wondered why Skye felt the need to reinforce what was already so thick on Bay's skin. The instinct to leave a scent felt very dog-like, and my lips fought against the smile the thought brought on. Skye's brow furrowed when his attention fell on my goofy face. "I've got eyes on Whisper, and she hasn't been followed, but she is stumbling through a Neverland forest at night, so we don't have time to waste."

Keeping high in the cover of fog, we darted for the forest, dropping in where a tree's branches met us in the sky. I peered through the shadows, hovering above the leaves and sticks until a mass of curly foliage shifted behind a bush. My nerves settled instantly.

"You made it," I breathed. "We all made it."

She jumped, turned, then peered above the bush at us, sighing at last. A small smile curved her lips. "Well, what took you both so long? I've been waiting here for *hours*."

"We were having too good a time." My eyes rolled. "And it was ten minutes at most."

Bay set a hand against my shoulder. "While your reunion is adorable, we actually need to keep moving. Hook's away getting the supplies he needs to invade Skyla, which means every pirate down there knows they are dead if he comes home to find us gone."

"Right. You already freed his bait. I don't want to be anywhere near him when he finds out you escaped too." Whisper looked behind her and stilled. I followed her gaze to find flickering lights blinking on past the boundaries of the trees. Torches. The search parties were already on the move.

"They're expert trackers, have to be to survive here." Bay's eyes narrowed. "Skye, you go with Wind Song and Whisper. I'll loop back after creating a couple false trails."

Skye's wings ruffled, but I spoke up first. "We're not splitting up. You can't even move your right arm right now. We'll have a better chance if we're together."

He threw a look through the trees at the approaching lights. "I'd argue, but we don't have time for that." Running his gaze over the ground, he nodded at a broken log. "How good is Whispering Meadow's balance?"

"This is the dumbest smart thing I have ever done." Whisper stared at the glowing log beneath her feet and clung to my arm while I flew beside her, guiding her after Bay and Skye. The log floated just above the ground, barely high enough to keep her from touching it and leaving a trail. "I kind of wish I didn't have to do it for hours, though."

"*She's* complaining?" Skye spun around her feet, dashed over my head, then returned to collapse on Bay's shoulder.

"We're almost there." Bay's voice was deep with the same exhaustion that I felt in my bones, and I hadn't been beaten nearly to death. "The Nixies guard their home, and they are terrifying creatures. We'll be safe within the bounds of the cove."

"Sorry. Are they terrifying or not?" Whisper's brow jumped, and her lips pursed as I moved her around a tree, ducking us beneath low-hanging branches.

"Same kind of terrifying as the sirens."

"Speaking of the sirens." Whisper's voice took on an air that made it clear if she could have, she would have folded her arms. "They saved our lives, gave us vital information and food, and have kept your mother safe for years. Why in the world were you running from them?"

Bay didn't reply immediately, and when he did, his answer was less than ideal. "Because they're nosy." Pausing, he turned with a frown. "*Speaking of,* what vital information are you talking about?"

"Oh, I don't know. Lyric's a demigod and the entire story of what happened between Hook and your mother." Whisper shifted, and I grappled for her, wondering if, at this point, the flying log method was really necessary.

Bay stared at us aghast. "They showed you that?"

"Well, they showed Lyric. I got the lovely abridged version."

"*Why* would they need to show you that?" He continued flying backwards before we caught up to him completely.

Truthfully, I didn't know exactly. Aside from fulfilling my curiosity, why had they thought I'd need to know what happened in a past they'd told me I couldn't change? "Sorry," I found myself saying, "I didn't really have a choice in the matter, but I didn't mean to invade your privacy or personal life."

"She told me you were an adorable kid. Where did all the pudge in your cheeks go?" Whisper's teasing had lost its filter, and I had half a mind to drop her on her ass when my cheeks flared red.

Skye scoffed. "Please, Bay's cuter now than he was as a brat, wouldn't you agree?" The pixie's smug little expression met my eye, and I was only spared by the fact Bay whirled around, mumbling reprimands.

Minutes passed, and the forest changed—entirely. I didn't even know when it happened. One moment, faded browns and greens surrounded us, then the next, blue and silver washed over trees heavy with blooms instead of leaves. Ponds, clear and sparkling, dabbled water pockets throughout the sparse trees.

I glanced over my shoulder, but it was too late. We were in the center of it.

And before us, a golden temple shot into the sky, the relic pulsing with magic. Shivers cut down my spine as I watched a hundred eyes snap open in the ponds. Yellow, blue, and glowing, they watched us from within scaly faces.

One of the creatures rose out of the water, her arms opened wide. "Welcome." Her voice shimmered. "We have been waiting for you."

Finish Lyric's story in Goddess of Air

A NOTE FROM THE AUTHOR

The Kingdom of Fairytales authors hope you enjoyed this new way of reading. We don't think that a series has ever been set with one chapter a day thought a whole year before and we hope we did it justice.

With this in mind, please leave a review, but when you do, remember that these books were always meant to be short breaks in your day and the blurb reflects that.

We would LOVE it if you can drop us a few words on Amazon

Review here

AFTER THE HAPPILY EVER AFTER...

There is more to these stories. You want to know what happens next right? Fast forward eighteen years...

Pick up book one now

PREQUEL

SLEEPING BEAUTY

1. Queen of Dragons
2. Heiress of Embers
3. Throne of Fury
4. Goddess of Flames

LITTLE MERMAID

5. Queen of Mermaids
6. Heiress of the Sea
7. Throne of Change
8. Goddess of Water

RED RIDING HOOD

9. King of Wolves
10. Heir of the Curse
11. Throne of Night
12. God of Shifters

RAPUNZEL

13. King of Devotion
14. Heir of Thorns
15. Throne of Enchantment
16. God of Loyalty

RUMPELSTILTSKIN

17. Queen of Unicorns
18. Heiress of Gold
19. Throne of Sacrifice
20. Goddess of Loss

BEAUTY AND THE BEAST

21. King of Beasts
22. Heir of Beauty
23. Throne of Betrayal
24. God of Illusion

ALADDIN

25. Queen of the Sun
26. Heiress of Shadows
27. Throne of the Phoenix
28. Goddess of Fire

CINDERELLA

29. Queen of Song
30. Heiress of Melody

31. Throne of Symphony
32. Goddess of Harmony

ALICE IN WONDERLAND

33. Queen of Clockwork
34. Heiress of Delusion
35. Throne of Cards
36. Goddess of Hearts

WIZARD OF OZ

37. King of Traitors
38. Heir of Fugitives
39. Throne of Emeralds
40. God of Storms

SNOW WHITE

41. Queen of Reflections
42. Heiress of Mirrors
43. Throne of Wands
44. Goddess of Magic

PETER PAN

45. Queen of Skies
46. Heiress of Stars
47. Throne of Feathers
48. Goddess of Air

URBIS

49. Kingdom of Royalty
50. Kingdom of Power
51. Kingdom of Fairytales
52. Kingdom of Ever After

JOIN US

Would you like to get Bay's adventure logs? Click the link below to pick your free gift up.

Kingdom of Fairytales FREE gift

Check the Kingdom of Fairytales website for competitions, news and info on all the books and authors

Kingdom of Fairytales Website

Or Join us on our Kingdom of Fairytales Facebook page for fun, games and author takeovers

Still want more? Completely immerse yourself in the Kingdom of Fairytales experience and pick up exclusive offers and gifts

Become a Patron

THE KINGDOM OF FAIRYTALES TEAM

These books would not be written without a great many people. Here is our team:

Many thanks to those who have made this possible.

Thank you to Rhi Parkes without whom, this series would never have come about.

Thanks to all the authors.

J.A. Armitage, Audrey Rich, B. Kristen Mcmichael, Emma Savant, Jennifer Ellision, Scarlett Kol, R. Castro, Margo Ryerkerk, Zara Quentin, Laura Greenwood and Anne Stryker

Also thank you to our amazing Beta team

Nadine Peterse-Vrijhof, Diane Major, Kalli Bunch and Stephanie Pittser.

Thanks to our Proof Reader

Tina Merritt

Thank you to our Patrons

Gigi Nickerson, Amanda Hurst & Coralee Butterfield

ABOUT J.A. ARMITAGE

J.A lives in a total fantasy world (because reality is boring right?) When she's not writing all the crazy fun in her head, she can be found eating cake, designing pretty pictures and hanging upside down from the tallest climbing frame in the local playground while her children look on in embarrassment. She's travelled the world working as everything from a banana picker in Australia to a Pantomime clown, has climbed to the top of Mount Kilimanjaro and the bottom of the Grand Canyon and once gave birth to a surrogate baby for a friend of hers.

She spends way too much time gossiping on facebook and if you want to be part of her Reading Army, where you'll get lots of freebies, exclusive sneak peeks and super secret sales, join up here

https://www.subscribepage.com/v7o8k4

Somehow she finds time to write.

ABOUT ANNE STRYKER

Anne Stryker was born and raised deep in the concrete garden of Jacksonville, Florida. As a Fantasy Romance author, Anne loves crafting fantastical worlds with swoony, humorous, or mysterious male leads and relatable main characters. Embracing the normal in the abnormal is her favorite pastime.

If you'd like to join her in her quest for Happily Ever Afters, you can find her on Instagram or you can join her Faerie Kaleidoscope by signing up to her mailing list:

Instagram: @AuthorAnneStryk
Faerie Kaleidoscope: http://eepurl.com/dGKJ6L